The Digest Enthusiast

Book Twelve

Michael Bracken

Steve Carper

Mike Chomko

Tony Gleeson

William Lampkin

Rick McCollum

Marc Myers

Michael Neno

Vince Nowell, Sr.

Rick Ollerman

John Shirley

Ward Smith

Bob Vojtko

Joe Wehrle, Jr.

Edited by Richard Krauss

The Digest Enthusiast (TDE) Book Twelve
Published twice a year by Larque Press LLC

Editor/Designer: Richard Krauss
Cover: by Tony Gleeson
Cartoons: Bob Vojtko (pages 45, 125)

Printed on demand from June 2020 in the United States of America
and other countries.

Larque Press LLC
4130 SE 162nd Court
Vancouver, WA 98683

Visit <larquepress.com> for news about current digest magazines and vintage digest covers. Join our mailing list for exclusive updates on *The Digest Enthusiast* and other Larque Press projects. Sign up at <larquepress.com>

Back Cover Images
Weirdbook No. 42 March 2020
The Adventures of Buffalo Bill by Col. William F. Cody
Science Stories No. 2 December 1953
Amazing Science Fiction Spec mockup by Tony Gleeson c. 1975
Fotocrime No. 2 February 1955
Amazing Stories Science Fiction Novel No. 1 1957

Our thanks to our contributors for some of the cover images that appear in this edition. Cover images are retouched to remove defects from the original source material. When reference material is not available, retouched areas are "best guess." In some cases text may be reset in a font similar to the original work.

Opposite: Digests sharing the newsstand with the debut issue of
Science Stories in October 1953 (page 96):
The Saint Detective Magazine Vol. 1 No. 4 Oct.-Nov. 1953
Fate Vol. 6 No. 10 (No. 43) October 1953
True Crime Detective Vol. 3 No. 4 Fall 1953
Weird Tales Vol. 45 No. 4 September 1953

The Digest Enthusiast
ISSN 2637-448X (print)
ISSN 2637-4498 (Kindle)
ISBN 978-1-7344548-2-6

Fantasy & Science Fiction May/June 2020. Cover by Maurizio Manzieri.

Fantasy & Science Fiction July/Aug 2020. Cover by Alan M. Clark.

News Digest

Gordon Van Gelder: Fantasy & Science Fiction

The July/Aug issue of *F&SF* is at the printer. It features stories by **M. Rickert**, **James Morrow**, **Mel Kassel**, **Rati Mehrota**, **Stephanie Feldman** and **Brian Trent**.

For our Sep/Oct issue, I just got **Bob Eggleton's** cover illustration for **David Gerrold's** "The Shadows of Alexandrium" and it's a knockout. The lineup for the issue isn't final yet but I think we're going to have a new Gorlen story by **Marc Laidlaw**, a novelet by **R. S. Benedict**, and a story by **Tim Powers** in the issue.

Jennifer Landles: Pulp Literature
Pulp Literature No. 26, Spring 2020

Tais Teng's Queen of Swords guards the gates to a new Erm Kaslo story from **Matthew Hughes**, mysteries deepen for Frankie Ray in **Mel Anastasiou's** "The Extra," and **JM Landels'** intrepid shepherdess Toinette arrives in Paris. We have short fiction from **Christi Nogle** and **Melisa Gregorio**, poetry from **Patti Pangborn** and **Sarah Summerson**, plus SiWC and Raven contest winners, and a short comic from **Rina Piccolo**.

Pulp Literature No. 27 Summer 2020

Savoury short fiction from **Tomson Highway**, **Jakob Drud**, **Kim Harbridge**, **Hannah Van Did-**

Pulp Literature No. 26 Spring 2020. Cover by Tais Teng.

Ellery Queen Mystery Magazine Mar/Apr 2019. Cover by Chris Clor.

Updates from the Editors, Writers, and Artists of today's newsstand and indie digest magazines.

den, and **R. Daniel Lester**. Further adventures of Frankie Ray in "The Extra" from **Mel Anastasiou** and a brand new Allaigna story from **JM Landels**. The winners of the Bumblebee Flash Fiction contest, a new comic from **Kris Sayer** and more!

Paul D. Marks: EQMM, etc.

Though I don't have any short stories in the immediate pipeline, some will be coming up, just no pub dates on them yet. My new novel, *The Blues Don't Care* drops on June 1, 2020 from Down & Out Books. New York Times best-selling author **Brendan DuBois** sums thing up like this: "On one level it's a mystery where a white musician, Bobby Saxon, in an all-black jazz band, works to solve a murder and clear his name under extraordinary racially-tinged circumstances. But this finely-written novel takes place in World War II-era Los Angeles, and Marks brings that long-gone era alive with memorable characters, scents, descriptions, and most of all, jazz. Highly recommended."

My short story "Fade-Out on Bunker Hill," from the March/April 2019 *Ellery Queen Mystery Magazine*, came in second in the magazine's 2020 Reader's Poll. For the online Quarantine-Stay-At-Home Awards Ceremony and speeches see <youtu.be/qWdoi_suC2Q>.

Finally, author **Frank Zafiro** grilled me for the Wrong Place, Write Crime podcast,

Analog May/June 2020.
Cover by Donato Giancola.

Analog July/August 2020.

episode 75 at <soundcloud.com/frank-zafiro-953165087/>.

Emily Hockaday: Analog

Analog continues our 90th anniversary strong with a retrospective story chosen by **Ben Bova** in July/August, **Sheila Williams** in September/October, and editor in chief **Trevor Quachri** in November/December. We'll also be publishing two exciting special features—an article on women in the magazine by **Marie Vibbert** and a look at how fact articles came to be a regular feature by **Edward M. Wysocki.**

Because we cannot gather in person to celebrate, *Analog* will be sharing a video presentation of the 2019 AnLab award winners, along with the *Asimov's* announcement of the readers' award winners. Readers can follow on social media to tune in.

Steve Darnall: Nostalgia Digest

Even as we observe social restrictions in a time of pandemic, the Summer 2020 issue of *Nostalgia Digest* offers fun in the sun with our all-new, all-vintage Swimsuit issue, featuring a full-color cover photo of **Barbara Stanwyck** and more than a dozen stars of stage, screen and radio—including **Doris Day**, **Ginger Rogers**, **Kirk Douglas**, **Jimmy Durante** (!) and others. The Summer issue of *Nostalgia Digest* also features a 60th anniversary celebration of *The Andy Griffith Show* and articles about **James Stewart**, **Jack Pearl** (radio's "Baron Munchausen"), baseball during World War II, a few moments with actor **Keir Dullea** and more!.

Although the Summer 2020 issue may be a bit harder to find in stores like Barnes & Nobel during the pandemic, issues will always be available directly from our website <nostalgiadigest.com>.

Nostalgia Digest Summer 2020. Cover with Barbara Stanwyck.

Michael Bracken: BCMM, Guns + Tacos, etc.

Issue 6 and the special private eye issue of *Black Cat Mystery Magazine* are in production and we hope to have both out soon.

Alfred Hitchcock's Mystery Magazine May/June 2020. Cover by Bastien Lecouffe Deharme.

The Best of Manhunt 2 edited by Jeff Vorzimmer. Stark House Press, 2020.

Issue No. 6 includes new stories by **Michael Bracken**, **Trey R. Barker**, **Patricia Dusenbury**, **Robert Guffey**, **John Hegenberger**, **Laird Long**, and **Robert Lopresti**, and a classic reprint by **Bryce Walton**. After reading through a great many submissions during last year's open call, we have accepted enough stories to fill issues 7–10. So, we don't expect to be reading submissions again until early to mid 2021.

Guns + Tacos, the serial novella anthology series I co-edit with **Trey R. Barker**, begins season two in July, with a novella released in ebook format each month for six months. All six novellas are later released in paperback. This season's contributors include **Ann Aptaker**, **Eric Beetner**, **Alec Cizak**, **Ryan Sayles**, **Mark Troy**, a collaboration by Trey and me, and a bonus story for subscribers only by Trey. Season three has already been ap-

proved by Down & Out Books.

My story "Caked" is scheduled for the June issue of *Thriller*, and, though I don't yet know in which issues they will appear, I have three stories forthcoming in *Alfred Hitchcock's Mystery Magazine*.

Janice Law: AHMM, BCMM, etc.

I have had a surprisingly good start to the year, with "The Client" in the May/June 2020 *AHMM* and "The Bodyguard" in the just released No.5 issue of *Black Cat Mystery Magazine*.

I recently sold stories to *AHMM* and *Sherlock Holmes Magazine*, the latter might interest Madam Salina readers as it features my new series character, the Holmes Impersonator, a mediocre actor who has a semi-steady gig impersonating the great man at the Sherlock Holmes Museum run by Dr. Jean Watson. I have also sold stories to

Asimov's May/June 2020. Cover by Anna & Elena Balbusso.

Asimov's July/August 2020.

two upcoming anthologies and am to have an Italian edition of *The Fires of London*, a Francis Bacon mystery.

Emily Hockaday: Asimov's

Asimov's looks forward to the rest of 2020 and the start of 2021 with stories from **Connie Willis**, **Kristine Kathryn Rusch**, **Greg Egan**, **Suzanne Palmer**, **Chen Quifan**, **Alaya Dawn Johnson**, **Ray Nayler**, **Nick Wolven**, and many other talented authors.

Rick McCollum: Pulp Modern, TDE

Rick posts daily updates worth firing up FB for every day. His WIPs include a comic book called *Wormwood* and two graphic novels that aren't likely to see print until 2021.

Jeff Vorzimmer: Manhunt and more

I've just wrapped up production on *The Best of Manhunt 2*, which is coming out August 17, 2020. I've also just finished editing and doing the layout on another **Gil Brewer** two-fer, *The Tease/Sin for Me* (July 24), with an introduction by **David Rachels**, the literature professor from Newberry College who is the foremost Brewer scholar.

The new Manhunt anthology clocks in at over 400 pages with 36 stories, all as good as in the first volume. There is a foreword by **Peter Enfantino**, and an introduction by the Anthony Award-winning author **Jon L. Breen**. Also in this edition we have article written in 1970 by the late great pulp writer **Robert Turner** titled "Life and Death of a Magazine," in which he chronicles his relationship with the magazine.

J.D. Graves: EconoClash Review, etc.

ECR No. 6 is better than UV or Bleach for curing those COVID Blues, and just as despicable.

EconoClash Review No. 6 edited by J.D. Graves..

Inside these pages monsters roam free. Some hide their oozing flesh and bloody claws inside skins draped with respectable clothes, firm haircuts, and bedroom teeth. Behold businessmen with carnival barker style and a gambler's desperation. Ride along in a bus filled with debauchery and regret. Search online paramours catfishing through dangerous mud. Sight in on the true costs of assassinations. Unleash unspeakable unknown under-dwellers. Discover buried treasure in the darkest depths of creation. Listen for the fluting call of spectral friends. Panic at the mention of No-Good Bartlett's. Float down a river of No Return. Oh, and there's also a time-traveling Jesus.

These nine quality cheap thrills of the dankest macabre and criminally petty, are guaranteed to delight your senses, tickle your outrage, and engorge your brain with blood. Read original stories by **Daniel Marcus, Preston Lang, Serena Jayne, John Kojak, Daniel Jacob Uitvlugt, Robb T. White, Paul McCabe, J.D. Graves,** and **Chris Fortunate** only in *EconoClash Review* six from Down & Out Books. Due: late June 2020.

Quarantine Quick Reads are cheap thrills published by Thrill Hill Bottom Press. The following titles are available for purchase on <Amazon.com>. "Just Another Job That Doesn't Pay Very Well,"

The Boy Detective & The Summer of '74 and Other Tales of Suspense by Art Taylor.

Ellery Queen Mystery Magazine May/June 2020. Cover by Neil Webb.

"The Sweetheart Sour," and "Her Coffin's Colder Than The Mink Glove." All written by **J.D. Graves**.

Robert Lopresti: AHMM

Robert makes his 31st appearance in *Alfred Hitchcock Mystery Magazine* with "Shanks Saves The World" in the May/June issue. He is back in the next issue with "The Library of Poisonville." He also has a story in *Low Down Dirty Vote* Volume II, out on the Fourth of July.

Art Taylor: AHMM, etc.

I've had a couple of stories published recently (and ahead) in anthologies, and one in *Alfred Hitchcock's Mystery Magazine* (Jan/Feb 2020) as well—the title story of my new collection, in fact: *The Boy Detective & The Summer of '74 and Other Tales of Suspense*—16 stories covering 25 years, published in Feb-ruary by Crippen & Landru. Other recent work includes: "A Close Shave," *The Swamp Killers*, a novel in stories (Down & Out Books, March 2020); "Both Sides Now," co-written with **Tara Laskowski** (my wife!), *The Beat of Black Wings: Crime Fiction Inspired by the Songs of Joni Mitchell* (Untreed Reads, April 2020); and "All Tomorrow's Parties," *Chesapeake Crimes: Invitation to Murder* (Wildside Press, forthcoming . . . this summer sometime?)

Josh Pachter: MWM, EQMM, AHMM, BCMM, D&O, etc.

The big news, of course, is that I just became the 2020 recipient of the Short Mystery Fiction Society's Edward D. Hoch Memorial Golden Derringer Award for Lifetime Achievement. I also won the "regular" Derringer for Best Flash Story of 2019, for "The Two-Body Problem,"

Mystery Weekly Magazine May 2020.
Cover by Robin Grenville Evans.

Mystery Weekly Magazine June 2020.
Cover by Robin Grenville Evans.

which appeared in the October 2019 issue of *Mystery Weekly*. This was the first time that a Golden Derringer recipient also won a competitive Derringer in the same year.

Recent publications? Let's see. "The Adventure of the Red Circles," second in my series of Ellery-Queen-and-the-Puzzle-Club pastiches, was in the Jan/Feb issue of *EQMM*, "The Pig is Committed" was in the April *Mystery Weekly*, and "The Beat of Black Wings" was in *The Beat of Black Wings: Crime Fiction Inspired by the Songs of Joni Mitchell* (Untreed Reads, April 2020), which I edited. I also edited *The Misadventures of Nero Wolfe* (Mysterious Press, April 2020) and co-edited *The Further Misadventures of Ellery Queen*, due any time now from Wildside Press. Finally, I translated Dutch author **Michael Berg's** "Travelers' Rest" for the May/June *EQMM*.

I have lots of stuff coming up: two new stories and two translations in *EQMM*, a translation in *AHMM*, new stories in *Black Cat Mystery Magazine* and *Mystery Tribune* and *Down and Out: The Magazine* and the new Sisters in Crime Chessie Chapter anthology *Invitation to Murder*. They say that, once you get a lifetime-achievement award, you should stop, already, but I'm not dead yet, and I have no intention of stopping. I just delivered the manuscript of a new anthology, *The Great Filling Station Holdup: Crime Fiction Inspired by the Songs of Jimmy Buffett*, which Down & Out will release next year, and now I'm working on *Only the Good Die Young: Crime Fiction Inspired by the Songs of Billy Joel* for Untreed Reads, due next April.

Chuck Carter: Mystery Weekly Monthly

Chuck was kind enough to share the cover of his June 2020 issue which features stories by

bare• bones No. 2 Spring 2020.

bare• bones No. 3 Summer 2020.

M.C. Tuggle, **Tammy Huffman**, **Robert Lopresti**, **Arthur Vidro**, **Allan Durand**, **Luke Foster**, **Carl Robinette**, and **Martin Hill Ortiz**. That troubled astronaut on the cover is a self-portrait of cover artist **Robin Grenville Evans**.

Peter Enfantino: bare•bones

bare•bones No. 2 is out at Amazon. Over 100 pages featuring a comprehensive look at The Sharpshooter men's adventure series; a never-published interview with **Richard Matheson** about his western novels; writer-director **S. Craig Zahler** on *The Spider* pulp; *TDE*'s **Richard Krauss** on *Mike Shayne*; *Shock Mystery Tales*; *Captain Action*; **David J. Schow**; sleaze novels; and much more. Issue 3 should be out by September and features a massive comparison of the original *Planet of the Apes* films and their paperback tie-ins.

Also in the works is a book with **Jose Cruz** on Harvey Pre-Code Horror Comics due in this Fall, and planned for Summer 2021, a volume focused on Atlas.

Scotch Rutherford: Switchblade

Switchblade No. 12 is due out in June and No. 13 is scheduled for September 2020.

Gary Lovisi: Paperback Parade

The next issue of *Paperback Parade* was all set for printing when Gary's printer closed down. As soon as they are back up and running, *PP* 107 will be printed and mailed to subscribers—perhaps even before you read these words. Gary also has an article on Falcon's digest-sized paperbacks ready for the next issue of *TDE*.

Phyllis Galde: Fate Magazine

"Losing **Rosemary Ellen Guiley**

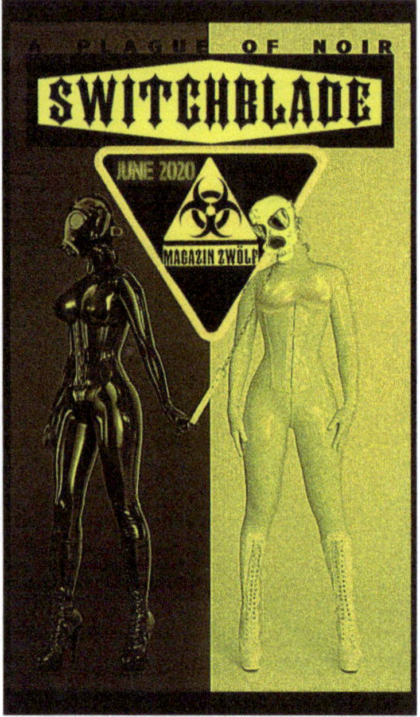

Switchblade No. 12 June 2020.

Paperback Parade No. 107 May 2020.

last July was a huge shock to me and the rest of the world!" Rosemary was *Fate*'s Executive Editor.

Fate No. 735 was released recently with articles on Tat-

Fate No. 735 ~May 2020.

toos, Shadow People, Devil's Footprints, Crystal Skulls, Spook Lights, Bees, and much more.

Visit the <fatemag.com> website for hefty savings on back issue lots and new *Fate* T-Shirts.

Steve Oliver: The Dark City

The April 2020 issue of *The Dark City Mystery Magazine* is out with stories by **James Blakey**, **Nicky Johnson**, **Michael Chandos**, **Roger Leatherwood**, and **Stef Donait**. The magazine is edited and published by **Steve Oliver**. Contributing editors are **Barbara Curtis** and **Darin Krogh**.

Rock and a Hard Place Magazine

Chronicles of bad decisions and desperate people. The second issue of *Rock and a Hard Place* was released in March 2020. Loaded with fiction, flash, essays, and art, this 148-page volume is led by Producing

The Dark Crime & Mystery Magazine
April 2020.

Rock and a Hard Place No. 2
Winter/Spring 2020.

Editor **Jonathan Elliott** and available in print and digital formats.

Rick Ollerman: Down & Out: The Magazine

As of early May, Rick was sourcing more stories to round out the next issue of *The Magazine*. Since there won't be a non-fiction column this time, there's more space for fiction. He also said, "I've bought stories from **Michael Bracken** before, and he just bought one from me for an anthology coming out next year, so we get to appear together in the same place for the first time—so that's cool.

"I have just about wrapped up the Bill Crider inspired anthology I've been working on (just got an intro from his daughter) and a few other things from my backlog have been wrapped up, and I did just agree to take on another book editing project."

Michael Neno: Comic Creator

I've been working on a series of public domain mashup micro comics I was going to be debuting at this year's Small Press and Alternative Comics Expo. Now that that show will be online only,

Horse Crime Comics by Michael Neno.

Hot Lead All Reviews Special May 2020. Edited by Justin Marriott.

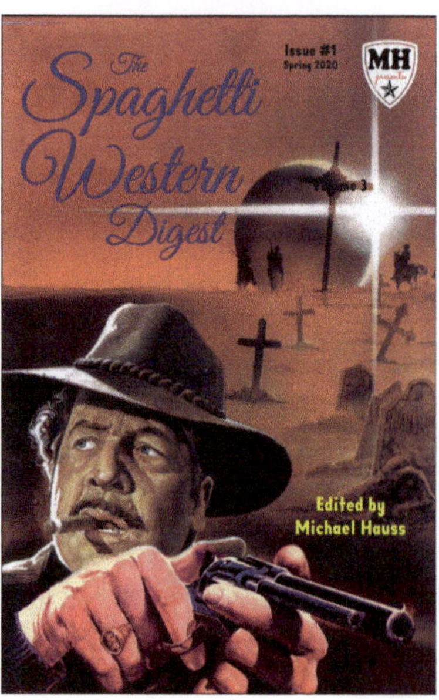

The Spaghetti Western Digest No. 1 Spring 2020. Edited by Michael Hauss.

I'll be offering the first title of that series, *Horse Crime Comics*, as a free digital download during the show, the weekend of July 11th at <nenoworld.com/Contents.html>.

Justin Marriott: Paperback Fanatic

Monster Maniacs No. 2, the journal of vintage horror in magazines, comics and fanzines has just been published (but been buried by Amazon, presumably as part of a COVID/reduced capacity response, so it needs finding). Eighty full colour pages of interviews, articles and reviews of monster mags and comics. Topics include *Web of Horror* magazine, Vampirella, **Tom Sutton's** work at Charlton, *Kevin O Neil's* early horror strip work, interviews with small press publishers of Deep Red, Midnight and Vampi. And more. Heavily illustrated.

Hot Lead All Reviews Special will be published by mid-May, 166 pages containing 215+ reviews of western paperbacks from 1929 to the modern day. Authors covered include **Louis L'Amour**, **Frank Gruber**, **Edgar Rice Burroughs**, **Harry Whittington**, **Elmore Leonard**, and special essays on the top 10 western authors and Gold Medal westerns.

In the Fall, one-off special *The Doomsday Warrior* will be published, a definitive guide to the men's adventure genre set in a post-apocalyptic world where red-blooded American freedom-fighters battled invading communists and blood-thirsty mutants. Reviews of series such as Deathlands, Mutants Amok, Phoenix, Traveler, The Last Ranger, Doomsday Warrior and more, plus interviews with authors such as **David Robbins** and **David Alexander**. This will be a blast!

Michael Hauss:
The Spaghetti Western Digest

The Spaghetti Western Digest is a new publication with 200 pages of interviews, articles, and reviews—richly embellished with photos, lobbies, and posters. The first issue was released in March 2020, with-writings by **Tom Betts** on his fabled fanzine *Westerns All'italiana*; **Dennis Capicik** looks at some obscure westerns; **Steve Fenton** reviews a fistful of oaters, and **Professor Van Roberts** writes about *A Bullet for the President* and *Requiem for a Gringo*. **Michael Hauss** looks at the western films of **Paolo Bianchini** along with **Eugenio Ercolani**. Also included are interviews with: **Eugenio Ercolani**, author of the book, *Darkening the Italian Screen: Interviews With Genre and Exploitation Directors Who Debuted in the 1950s and 1960s*, **Javier Ramos**, co-author of *Cine del Oeste en la Comunidad de Madrid* and composer/director **Chuck Cirino**. **Steve Fenton** also shares a never before published interview with **Brett Halsey**, along with a detailed bio of Halsey. The goal is to publish *The Spaghetti Western Digest* four times a year. The digest is 6" x 9" and is available for $12.99 on <amazon.com>. Issue one's cover designer, **Tim Paxton** (*Monster!*), is also onboard for the second issue, planned for a Sept. 2020 release.

Acknowledgments
My thanks to readers and contributors for your support. Many of the enthusiasts who helped spread the word about *TDE11* follow. All comments and ratings are greatly appreciated. My apologies if I've missed anyone.

Blog Posts/Newsletters
Paul D. Marks <pauldmarks.com>
Pulp Literature <pulpliterature.com>
James Reasoner <jamesreasoner.blogspot.com>
Stark House Press <starkhousepress.com>
Bill Thom <PulpComingAttractions.com>
John O'Neill <blackgate.com>

Booksellers
Bud's Art Books
Mike Chomko Books

Ratings/Reviews/Tweets/Listings
Steve Alcorn, Dawn, J.D. Graves, Karl, Keith, Michael Neno, Janice Trecker, Jeff Vorzimmer, and rêveur d'art.

Social Media Posts, Shares, and Likes
(Facebook, etc.)
Bob Bailey, Ashok Banker, Trey R. Barker, Leslie Berry, Jack Bertram, Verl Bond, Ben Boulden, Michael Bracken, Mary Burgess, Michael Anthony Carroll, Steve Carper, C.F. Carter, Steve Cooper, Alec Cizak, Bob Corby, Elizabeth Crowens, Clark Dissmeyer, Peter Enfantino, Jonathan Falk, Brad W. Foster, Canada Keck, Bob Keller, Rachel Krauss, Tony Gleeson, Tim Goebel, Matthew Gomez, John Linwood Grant, J.D. Graves, John Haines, Bruce Harris, Adam House, John Hull, David Hyman, John Kojak, George A. Lane III, Robert Lopresti, Amy Marks, Paul D. Marks, Stan McCauley, Rick McCollum, Bryan Moose, Ron Morreale, William Patrick Murray, David Nemeth, Mary Neno, Michael Neno, Kathleen Banks Nutter, Drew O'Neill, Josh Pachter, William Dylan Powell, Maria Schrater, Victor Scott, Jim Shaffer, Kipp Poe Speicher, Duane Spurlock, Bill Thom, Benjamin Thomas, S.J. Thompson, Sally Tibbetts, Kevin Tipple, Prashant C. Trikannad, Albert Tucher, Edd Vick, David Vineyard, Bob Vojtko, Jeff Vorzimmer, Pierce Waters, Bill Widener, and Cindy Woods.

Final cover for *Pulp Modern* No. 5 by **Rick McCollum**, along with three preliminary "sketches." *PM5* includes stories by **Andrew Bourelle**, **"Doc" Clancy**, **Timothy Friend**, **Adam S. Furman**, **Nils Gilbertson**, **Peter W.J. Hayes**, **Serena Jayne**, **Mandi Jourdan**, and **Victoria Weisfeld**. Interior art by **Ran Scott**. Edited by **Alec Cizak**.

Guns + Tacos Season One
Created/Edited by Michael Bracken and Trey R. Barker
Review by Richard Krauss

Guns + Tacos follows the model of an independent video series. Season One, was released to subscribers in a series of ebooks, each by a different author. When the season ended, Down & Out Books collected them all in print, in a two volume set.

You have to love this series' premise: "There's a taco truck in Chicago known among a certain segment of the population for its daily specials. Late at night and during the wee hours of the morning, it isn't the food selection that attracts customers, it's the illegal weapons available with the special order. Each episode of Guns + Tacos features the story of one Chicagoland resident who visits the taco truck seeking a solution to life's problems, a solution that always comes in a to-go bag."

Guns + Tacos Season One
Volume One
Tacos de Cazuela con Smith & Wesson by Gary Phillips

Augustina "Gus" Blanchard is a doctor by day. Assisted by nurse Ursula Marsh, the two are all business at the hospital. But the pair are deeply involved on the down low. Why does Blanchard need a Smith & Wesson? She's out to avenge the death of her brother and she has all the skills of a finely-tuned Wonder Woman. When she drugs big shot Dr. Broderick Freslan, he reveals the location of his secret lab and things turn wild. The action barely pauses to breathe in this modern day weird menace mash-up.

Three Brisket Taco and a Sig Sauer
by Michael Bracken

Joey and his aunt Sylvia are partners in crime and surprisingly share the same bed too. She's only slightly

older than her toy-boy due to a seriously botched familial tree. It ain't love, it's brains and brawn—using "brains" in its broadest application. Likewise, for "stupid" Joey, who holds his own on everything except the big picture—and the relationship between cause and effect.

Joey got caught in a robbery in progress and did a short bit while Sylvia got out the back door with the cash. Fresh out of stir, Joey picks up a Sig Sauer at the taco truck to prep for Syliva's latest brainstorm—bank robbery. There are a few dicey sub-plots wrapped around the wheelset of this runaway train but—no worries—they all unspool by the time the gun smoke clears.

A Gyro and a Glock by Frank Zafiro

In the world of junkies what Tim and Ernie had was something rare. "People in our world tended to concern themselves with looking out for number one. Sure, there were partnerships. The business variety

happened all the time, but they were fragile and temporary, lasting only as long as the money was good and the risk or the cost was low enough." But Tim and Ernie were different. They weren't lovers, or even brothers, yet their loyalties ran that deep.

Life was good. As good as petty crimes, dive joints, and shooting up can get. Then officer Musgrave came calling. He got his claws into Tim, turned him into a stoolie, and that looked like the end of that. But, everything changed when Tim stopped by Jesse's taco trunk and ordered the special.

Guns + Tacos Season One Volume Two

Three Chalupas, Rice, Soda…and a Kimber .45 by Trey R. Barker

The perfect crime is a myth. There are unsolved crimes. There are crimes without convictions. But every crime leaves a mark. Victims of minor crimes can recover. But victims of major crimes will always feel their scars. The unidentified Sergeant in "Kimber" is an internet exploitation investigator driven by a tragedy of his youth. His manic doggedness baiting sex offenders alienates everyone around him, and Barker illustrates the detective's skewed sensibilities by masterfully telling his story from the intimate distance of second person.

Some Churros and El Burro
by William Dylan Powell

A self-taught IT tech, who works for the Sangre Cartel down Mexico way, is tasked with troubleshooting an upstart ecstasy distributor in Chi-town. Chispa may be green, but he's smart. Other than the ice and cold, he likes what he sees in the Windy City, particularly the university and its massive library. Ideally, he wants to shut down the competition and then figure out a way to quit the Cartel. Too bad he only has two days to get the job done.

A Beretta, Burritos, and Bears
by James A. Hearn

"It had been a twisted trail from a happy home life to ex-con. Before his arrest, Brian would have described his life as perfect. He had a gorgeous wife, a faithful dog named Buster, and a modest home in a quiet suburban neighborhood west of Chicago. His job as a deliveryman for Schwartz's Office Emporium was nothing to write home about, but it paid the bills." The twisted tale begins when the drug enforcement squad pulls over Brian's delivery van and finds 5,000 grams of marijuana—4,970 grams over the legal limit. By the time he's lawyered up, Brian finds himself facing a three year bit and good reason to order the special from Jessie's taco truck.

Volume Two includes a short bonus story for series' subscribers: Episode 6-1/2:

Platanos con Lechera and a Snub-Nosed .38 by Michael Bracken

A former hitman goes all in on a final job on account of the recent misalignment of the stars. Apparently, what they need to set them straight is a good whack.

Guns + Tacos Season One from Down & Out Books is a terrific collection of hardboiled fiction that leans heavily into noir territory. Highly recommended.

J. Grant Thiessen published the second issue of *The Science-Fiction Collector* zine in 1976. Its article, "Gone But Not Forgotten: Indexes to defunct paperback lines," includes several digest-sized paperbacks that complement coverage in Vince Nowell, Sr.'s article on page 126. A PDF of *The Science-Fiction Collector* No. 2 is available at <efanzines.com>.
Thanks to Steve Carper for the tip.

Tony Gleeson

Interviewed by Richard Krauss
Conducted via email in February 2020

The Digest Enthusiast: I'm familiar with your illustration work for *Fantastic* and *Mike Shayne*. What other digest magazines have featured your work?

Tony Gleeson: Just as an overview, when I first started my hopeful career as an ink-stained wretch in NYC in the mid-70s, I did a fair amount of work for the SF digests, notably *Amazing* and *Fantastic*. I also did a piece for James Baen at *Galaxy*—to his specifications—that never saw print. As the result of that work I got a number of cover commissions from the Science Fiction Book Club and began doing a lot of painted illustrations for magazines and book publishers. By that time I had moved to Los Angeles. and that was the period when I did the *Mike Shayne* cover. Through the 1980s, I did extensive editorial illustration for various small publishers:

books, mags, newspapers. The *L. A. Times* published my stuff. I did educational material, packaging art, lots of ad illustrations of food and products, and stuff. Catalog drawings. Storyboarding. Concept art for TV, film, ads, toys, theme parks. I did anything I could, experimenting in different styles and media. I just wanted to be able to keep working in a profession that was quite challenging even for talents far more accomplished than myself (many of whom moved out of illustration into art direction, graphic design, or unrelated fields). Throughout the 1990s, I worked as a staff artist for Neal Adams Continuity Studios while continuing to run my own studio. As the new millennium broke, I found a niche doing illustration for a whole bunch of independent newspapers around the country. At last count, I've had something like a thousand illustrations printed in various places. I like to say I'm the most-published artist you probably haven't heard of!

TDE: You have an impressive resume! How did make your first connection into the world of SF digests?

TG: When I departed art school (Art Center here in L.A.) and headed to New York in early 1974, my first forays were to the various comics publishers and science fiction publishers, among other book and magazine companies. I was getting a lot of doors shut in my face, but almost always very politely. I was living in an apartment in Flushing, Queens, spending every day either constantly drawing and painting to create new samples or getting on the train to head to Manhattan to pound more pavement. One day I noticed on the masthead of *Amazing Science Fiction* (or maybe it was their "sister publication" *Fantastic Stories*) that it was published by "Ultimate Publishing" with a Flushing address! I looked up their

phone number and called and got a rather short and officious reply to just send in my samples. By this point I was getting unsatisfied with being turned down so I decided to put my portfolio together and get on a bus

Gleeson's first artwork for *Amazing Science Fiction* illustrating David Skal's "The Spirit of Seventy Six" December 1974.

to Ultimate Publishing, which was a few short miles away. I had this image of a publishing office in an office building, with secretaries and editors and art directors bustling around. Hey, I was, like, 24. So when the bus let me off in the middle of a distinctly residential Queens neighborhood, I was a little confused. As it turns out, the address on the masthead was the home of publisher Sol Cohen. I would later discover that some of the other names on the masthead were fictitious; Sol and Ted [White] basically put out the mags, communicating back and forth from New York and Virginia. I had a lot to learn about the reality of the "magazine world," as one art director later put it.

I wasn't really sure what I should do, so I walked back and forth up and down the street for a long time, screwing up my courage, and finally said, hang it all, marched up the porch steps and rang the bell. An older guy in a wife beater yanked open the door and said something like, "What do you want?" It was Sol. Somehow I got him to ask me in and to look at my work. He spread it out on his living room coffee table, which is probably where he did all the pasteups and camera ready art for the mags. I was pretty terrified, but there I was. Finally he said something I shall never forget: "Well, you're good, no getting around that. Maybe I've got something for you." Maybe he just admired my chutzpah, but that same week, he called me up to ask me if I'd do a piece for the December 1974 *Amazing*: "The Spirit of 76" by David Skal. I must have labored and agonized unendingly on that one. I got back on the same bus and dropped it off to him and he gave me a check then and there. It was insanely low, but I didn't care: it was a foot finally in the door.

Curiously, Sol called me back not long thereafter and asked if I could quickly knock out a second piece for the same issue since it looked as if Steve Fabian's art wasn't going to arrive on time. So I worked up art for Brian Stableford's "An Offer of Oblivion," but it never got used because, I guess, Fabian's art did arrive after all. But thereafter, Sol did call me pretty much every month with another piece for *Amazing* or *Fantastic*. I've heard stories of his infamous curmudgeonliness but I must say, he and I got along very well. I guess he never forgot my being a mensch and knocking on his door cold.

When I met my wife-to-be and moved to Manhattan, and then later to California, I continued to get calls from him for monthly illustrations but now I'd mail them in. My one regret, perhaps, was I never got the full-page space for the lead story that seemed to be Steve Fabian's birthright every month. Those long skinny half-page illustrations were a constant design challenge. I even submitted a few cover paintings, which I think would have been pretty good, but for some reason he never went with any of them. After Sol sold his interest to his partner Arthur Bernhard and *Amazing* moved to Arizona, I continued to do some pieces for their editor/art director, Elinor Mavor (a marvelous and interesting lady with whom I am still friends today). All in all I did maybe 50 illustrations for *Amazing* and *Fantastic*. I still look upon them as an invaluable experience

Gleeson's illustration for Vsevolod Ivanov's "Sisyphus, Son of Aeolus" translated by John W. Andrews for *Fantastic* December 1975.

Gleeson's illustration for Grania Davis' "New-Way-Groovers Stew" for *Fantastic* August 1976.

and education in so many ways.

I did show my work to James Baen [Editor] of *Galaxy* in the 70s as well. He seemed quite interested in my work and asked if I'd do a full-page piece for the magazine's "artist showcase" (or whatever they called it). He went to the trouble to excitedly conjure up the kinds of stuff he'd like to see: classic science fiction with bug-eyed monsters and machinery. I put together something that I still think is a wacked-out wonder to this day, and he seemed pretty jazzed about it. That was the last I ever heard from him. Maybe a year or two later I got a call from a bored-sounding secretary asking, "So are you gonna come pick up your artwork, or what?" It was, to my knowledge, never published—I've never seen it and I never got paid for it—and I still have the original which has paid its rent in various other ways over the years. I'm told it was one of the pieces that convinced Neal Adams to hire me many years later.

TDE: You were in good company among the artists in those magazines. Did you ever meet any of them?

TG: I did encounter Jeff Jones a few times, just casually to chat briefly at shows, which was a thrill for me. Despite the fact we were rather close in age, Jeff was a major influence and inspiration on my early work, thanks to our mutual friend Larry Ivie, who had made me aware early on of the amazing, brilliant out-of-the-gate work of my contemporary. I was fortunate enough to have more extensive online conversations with Jeffrey Catherine Jones in her final years that were quite cordial, if not exactly deep. I at least got the chance to express my appreciation to her.

I never did meet any of the other artists whose work appeared in those issues, though. We were pretty isolated in the process. I would have loved to be able to have a chat with Steve Fabian especially in those days.

I have had the opportunity to meet a few of the authors whose stories I illustrated, such as David Skal (in person) and the late Grania Davis (online). I brought a copy of "Spirit of Seventy Six" to a signing David was doing and I think I took him by surprise with that blast from his early career. He's not "Dave" anymore, for one thing….

TDE: What was the process for a typical assignment?

TG: As long as Sol was publisher, he would call me and ask if I was available to do a new story and then (as of late 1975 when I moved out of Queens) would send a photocopy of the story galley to me. If memory serves, he even called me after I moved to California in 1977, but he certainly continued to send me the galleys. There was never any discussion of the story or what the illustration should have in it. I simply read the story and went right to a final piece. There were no preliminaries; I just sent back the finished drawings. I'm guessing he worked that way with all the artists due to the short turnaround time and the low rates involved. Whether or not it was his intention, I felt I was given a good deal of confidence that I was going to come up with a good solution month after month. Working without a net, to be sure, and on occasion I'm afraid it showed (all of us have work we think is better than other

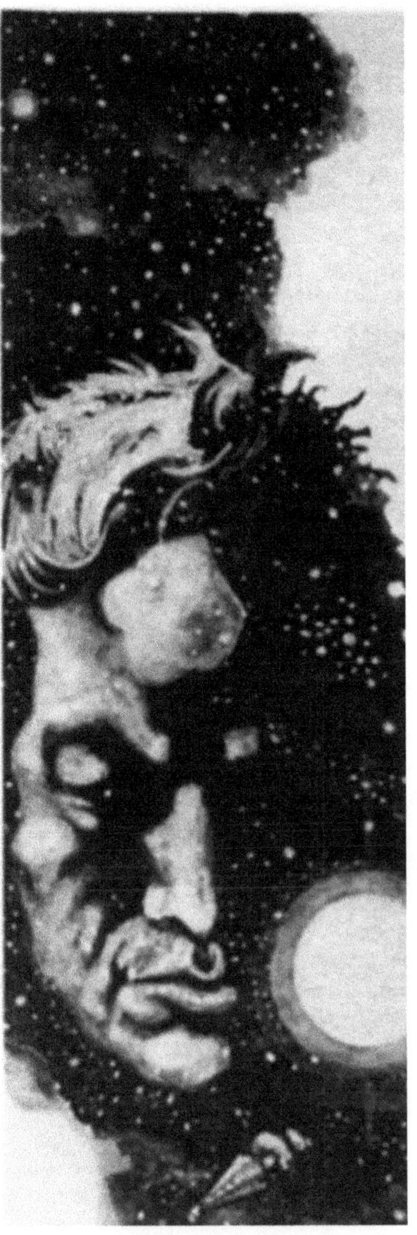

Gleeson's illustration for Dennis R. Bailey and David Bischoff's "Tin Woodman" for *Amazing* December 1976.

Gleeson's illustration for Joseph F. Pumila and Steve Utley's "Our Vanishing Triceratops" for *Amazing* March 1977.

work we've done). But it was a very good hands-on laboratory for me. I was allowed some leeway to take chances, some of which worked and some of which didn't, and I learned how to make choices while working.

It was a somewhat different process from most of the illustration jobs I'd subsequently take on, where there was quite a bit more in the way of personal communication, art direction, sketches and preliminaries, and art revisions. On the other hand, those subsequent jobs paid somewhat better too, so it was a tradeoff. One thing I did adopt as a policy (and continue to this day) was to thoroughly read anything I was being asked to illustrate: story, article, book, whatever. It meant I could approach the job in a reasonably intelligent fashion. One time the Science Fiction Book Club assigned me five book covers at once and they sent me all five books—and I read them all before starting!

Something I only learned many years later in a correspondence with Ted White, which was the first time he and I had ever "met"; he told me he was also active in deciding the illustration assignments for *Fantastic* and *Amazing*, that it hadn't just been Sol's decision as to who got what. He seemed a bit surprised, in fact, that I had been laboring under that delusion all those years.

Those were the years of the so-called New Wave in science fiction and I was often called upon to illustrate a story that was very "heady" and edgy, which could present a challenge for a concept image. It wasn't uncommon for one of my relatives or friends to call me up, having picked up one of the mags, and say, "Uh, nice drawing, but what in blazes was that story about? I didn't get it!" I'm okay with "think pieces" and I think I succeeded most of the time and fell on my face once in a while. Then I'd find myself assigned a S&S tale in *Fantastic* by Lin Carter or a similar author and could do something concrete.

When Arthur Bernhard and Elinor Mavor took over the reins of *Amazing*, in 1979, she contacted me by mail and we continued working together for a short time in pretty much the same way. She would send me a story, and I'd send her a finished piece. One big difference was that she formatted the magazine differently and now I got to do two-page spreads and to have some fun with the layout. She was a good designer and could work the layout of the page around an oddly configured illustration, so we had some fun in the short time we worked together.

Oh yeah, I pretty much always got the originals sent back to me. I still possess a number of them. Some of them are now in the collections of other folks.

TDE: Did you receive copies of the magazines?

TG: Sol never sent comps; I always had to hunt the mag down on the newsstand which in those days thankfully were all over. I don't remember if Elinor sent me comps after she took over. She very well might have.

TDE: As wonderful as it must have been to have a steady demand for your artwork for these digests, they couldn't have paid your way. What other work were you doing to support yourself during this period, and how did you fit these into your schedule?

TG: Oh, they clearly did not pay

Gleeson's illustration for Lin Carter's "The Pillars of Hell" for *Fantastic* December 1977.

my way. More they were one of the ways of expressing the imaginative side of my work, and also they allowed me to experiment with styles and concepts. In New York, I had a full-time job with a graphic design studio. It was mostly production work, the old-fashioned kind: paste pots, X-Acto knives, rubylith overlays and so forth. Surprisingly, the skills I developed there translated over into my drawing and painting and helped give me a lot more precision and care. I also met a number of clients there for whom I would do freelance illustration, mostly advertising type stuff. All my freelance work, of course, was done evenings and weekends. It was an adventure to learn the various ways to see clients, do on-site work when necessary, and deliver finishes, all sandwiched in with giving my full-time employer the time and work he rightly expected.

I sometimes met with my freelance clients during my lunch break, and now and then would have to have a phone conversation during my regular gig, and a couple of times there were awkward moments because of that. It's all part of the game: you learn how to do stuff like that. By the way, most studios kind of understand that you're doing side gigs and as long as you're discreet and responsible about your commitment to them and it's not a distraction, they'll look the other way.

When we moved to California, I jumped into freelancing whole hog. Luckily, my wife, who is an RN, had full time employment and was willing to help us through the tough periods. After the expected rough start, I began to get various kinds of work. Some of my very earliest work came from art school friends who had landed in the music business and pointed me into doing compre-

Tony Gleeson's artwork in *Amazing Science Fiction*

- [ ] Vol. 48 No. 4 December 1974 "The Spirit of Seventy Six" by David J. Skal
- [ ] Vol. 48 No. 6 May 1975 "Dominion" by Ken Wisman
- [ ] Vol. 49 No. 1 July 1975 "The Way of Our Fathers" by Daphne Castell
- [ ] Vol. 49 No. 2 September 1975 "Deliveryman" by Richard E. Peck
- [ ] Vol. 49 No. 3 November 1975 "Heel" by Richard E. Peck
- [ ] Vol. 49 No. 4 January 1976 "The Computer Cried Charge!" by George R.R. Martin
- [ ] Vol. 49 No. 5 March 1976 "Stone Circle" by Lisa Tuttle
- [ ] Vol. 50 No. 1 June 1976 "Ghur R'Hut Urr" by Robert F. Young
- [ ] Vol. 50 No. 2 September 1976 "Mrs. T" by Lisa Tuttle
- [ ] Vol. 50 No. 3 December 1976 "Tin Woodman" by Dennis R. Bailey and David Bischoff
- [ ] Vol. 50 No. 4 March 1977 "Our Vanishing Triceratops" by Joseph F. Pumila and Steve Utley
    "Those Thrilling Days of Yesteryear" by Jack C. Haldeman, II
- [ ] Vol. 50 No. 5 July 1977 "Social Blunder" by Tom Godwin
- [ ] Vol. 51 No. 2 January 1978 "The Looking Glass of the Law" by Kevin O'Donnell, Jr.
- [ ] Vol. 51 No. 3 May 1978 "All Things to All…" by Mack Reynolds
    "Charioteer" by Steve Miller
- [ ] Vol. 51 No. 4 August 1978 "Catalyst" by Charles V. De Vet
    "Tween" by J.F. Bone
- [ ] Vol. 52 No. 1 Nov. 1978 "Doggy in the Window" (John Grimes) by A. Bertram Chandler
    "Ponce" by Glen Cook
- [ ] Vol. 53 No. 1 November 1979 "The White Ones" by Wayne Wightman
- [ ] Vol. 53 No. 2 February 1980 "Mushroom Farmers" by Kurt von Stuckrad

hensive layout designs for LP covers and things like that. Luckily the Science Fiction Book Club took an interest in me (largely as the result of my work for the digests) and started sending me assignments doing art for their covers and for their promotional brochure. That was a big break. I started getting book cover work here in Los Angeles as well. Then I hooked up with a few local publishers who did magazines and paperbacks, and some educational

The illustration Gleeson drew for James Baen for *Galaxy* that never saw print in the magazine.

companies who put out enormous amounts of material and needed a lot of art, and for a few years they flooded me with stuff so I was working pretty regularly. I also got to do a lot of art for various departments of the *Los Angeles Times*.

Since we're focusing on the period where I was working for the digests, I'll not expound on anything past 1980, when I did the *Mike Shayne* cover (and at which point I had ceased contributing to *Amazing*), but suffice to say being an ink-stained wretch was never easy. It was a great ride, with lots of ups and downs and immense satisfaction, but not easy. I think the idea that runs through all of this is, if you really want to be an illustrator, expect to work a lot. You better absolutely love what you're doing because you're going to be doing it all the time. You better have no great love of the idea of weekends or evenings as a respite from work. Sometimes your "weekend" will come on, say, a Tuesday. Sometimes your time to snooze will be ten A.M. after working twelve hours. And if you truly love it, it will be very satisfying indeed.

TDE: Looks like you used zip-a-tone on some of your drawings for Sol Cohen, so your skills cutting rubylith and amberlith transferred smoothly into your illustration work.

TG: I did a fair amount of that early on. Larry Ivie, who I hung out with a little when I first got to New York, kept trying to get me to stop using it on my comic pages and illustrations. He thought it was lazy and limiting: his argument was that I should be learning how to get mid-tones without the "Ben Day" crutch. I still think I used it pretty judiciously. Over time, I tried to use stippling and other kinds of line shading for the midtones . . . or, on occasion, I'd try a painting with blacks, whites and greys, once I learned the mags were willing to run halftones if necessary. Once or twice

Tony Gleeson's artwork in *Fantastic Stories*

- [ ] Vol. 24 No. 3 April 1975 "Emptying the Plate" by Ross Rocklynne
- [ ] Vol. 24 No. 4 June 1975 "Goodbye Joe Quietwater—Hello!" by Williams Nabors
- [ ] Vol. 24 No. 5 August 1975 "Transfer" by Barry N. Malzberg
- [ ] Vol. 24 No. 6 October 1975 "From Bondeen to Ramur" by W.S. Doxey
- [ ] Vol. 25 No. 1 December 1975 "Sisyphus, Son of Aeolus" by Vsevolod Ivanov, translated by John W. Andrews
- [ ] Vol. 25 No. 3 May 1976 "Limits" by Jack Haldeman and Jack Dann
- [ ] Vol. 25 No. 4 August 1976 "New-Way-Groovers Stew" by Grania Davis
- [ ] Vol. 25 No. 5 November 1976 "Black Moonlight" (Thongor) by Lin Carter
- [ ] Vol. 26 No. 1 February 1977 "Miasmas—A life Term" by William Nabors
- [ ] Vol. 26 No. 2 June 1977 "The Earth Books" by Robert F. Young
- [ ] Vol. 26 No. 3 September 1977 "Indigestion" by Barry N. Malzberg
- [ ] Vol. 26 No. 4 December 1977 "The Pillars of Hell" by Lin Carter "Visitors" by Jack Dann
- [ ] Vol. 27 No. 1 April 1978 "Nemesis Place" by David Drake "The Golden Fleece" by Arsen Damay
- [ ] Vol. 27 No. 2 July 1978 "David's Friend, The Hole" by Grania Davis
- [ ] Vol. 27 No. 3 October 1978 "Demon and Demoiselle" by Janet Fox "Tahiti in Terms of Squares" by John Shirley
- [ ] Vol. 27 No. 4 "A Sense of Disaster?" by Christopher Anvil "Birds of the Moon" by Lisa Tuttle

One of two paintings Gleeson submitted to Cohen for *Amazing* covers. The other is featured on the cover of this issue of *The Digest Enthusiast*.

Gleeson's illustration for Jack Dann's "Visitors" for *Fantastic* December 1977.

I experimented with markers to get the midtones! But sometimes that perhaps confused Sol, who I believe did all the pre-print production, and had unintended results. Once he ran a painting of mine in line and it looked, well, dark and bizarre. Another time or two he'd run a line drawing in halftones, which wasn't all that bad although it tended to make the blacks wash out into greys.

TDE: I remember Larry Ivie for his *Monsters and Heroes* magazine.

TG: Larry was one of my first and oldest art teachers. I guess he was my version of the Famous Artists School. We carried on a correspondence from the time I was about 13 or 14 (resulting from a letter I sent to *Castle of Frankenstein* magazine) and he sent me scads of excellent art lessons for many years. I credit him for instilling in me the appreciation for a deep understanding and constant study of anatomy. We remained friends over time and were still corresponding a year or two before his death.

TDE: Leo Margulies moved Renown Publications from New York to Los Angeles late in 1972. Did you connect with him or someone else for your *Mike Shayne* work?

TG: Alas, I never had the opportunity to meet or work with the legendary Mr. Margulies. I believe he passed away in 1975. My brief association with *Mike Shayne Mystery Magazine* took place in 1980, by which time Eddie Goldstein was the publisher and Chuck Fritch the editor. In the late 70s in Los Angeles, one of the areas I found quite fertile for illustration was the "adult publication" market, mostly magazines that were *Playboy* wannabes, with varying pretensions to respectability. Basically, I drew a lotta "artsy" naked women, but just as often I also illustrated straightforward articles and stories. In the course of getting that kind of work, I encountered Eddie and his wife Anita, who published a whole bunch of different things. Much of what they did would be considered "adult" but they had also acquired Renown Publications by that point. They were always very cordial to me and quite a pair of characters. I would knock out several dozen drawings and come home with a fairly nice check on the spot for the week's work. They employed several writers who, like me, were just in search of a gig (some would go on to higher profile things). Eddie and Anita would invite us in to discuss the work we had all just brought in; Anita would sweetly offer me cookies while we talked about somewhat adult topics. One day Eddie mentioned he published *Mike Shayne*, and would I be interested in doing cover art? Of course I was, so he escorted me back to Chuck Fritch's office to introduce us. Chuck immediately said, "Gleeson . . . I've got a writer by that name, Paul Gleeson . . . any relation?" It was my elder brother, who was an attorney by profession but on the side wrote lots of splendidly quirky crime and horror stories that reflected the EC comics that he and I had grown up reading. He had started submitting them to various magazines and, as it turned out, *Shayne* was the only venue that ever bought a couple of them. Chuck thought this was a marvelous hook and ran a story of Paul's along with my cover painting. In his "Mystery Makers" profiles for

Gleeson's illustration for Kevin O'Donnell, Jr.'s "The Looking Glass of the Law" for *Amazing* January 1978.

Mike Shayne Mystery Magazine May 1980 with Paul Gleeson's "Unhappy Hour."

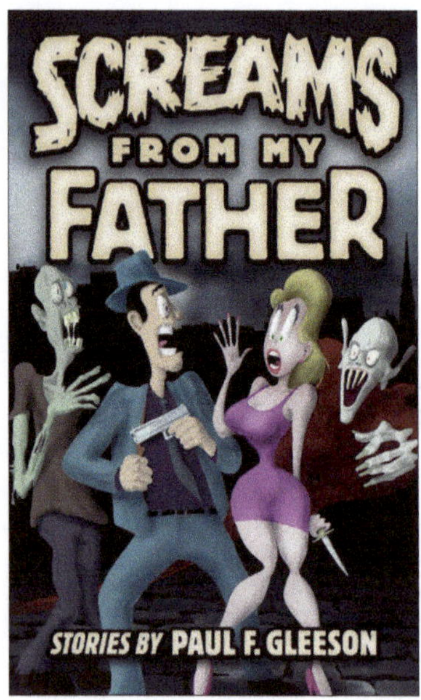

Screams from My Father by Paul Gleeson, cover by Brendan Gleeson 2014

that issue he proclaimed, "We've got a brother-brother act in this issue."

As memory serves, I didn't have a lot of turnaround time, maybe a day or two. Chuck needed something in a hurry. He specified a fistfight with some mayhem, some nasty thugs, and of course a pneumatic young woman. To my eyes, the painting I submitted reflects that it was rushed, but Chuck gave me the definite impression he liked it, and I've gotten good feedback on it over the years, so, I guess everybody sees things in differing lights.

I believe I continued to do some artwork for Eddie for a while after that, but that kind of market was evanescent for many reasons and tended to dry up suddenly. I'm not sure why I didn't do any further work for Chuck or for *Shayne*. That one cover was fun but I would have liked to have had another shot with more time to really get

into it. As I said earlier, doors tend to close up without notice.

TDE: Was that your final work for digests? You mentioned EC comics, did you ever do any comic book stories?

TG: *Shayne* was my last work for the classic digests. I did a number of paperback covers in the early 80s (one of my clients was the legendary Holloway House!) and another couple of pieces for the Science Fiction Book Club, but the market for my painting slowly ebbed and I found myself doing many other kinds of illustration and art.

I did a small amount of comic book work, never did get to work for any of the majors like DC, Marvel, Dark Horse, etc. In 1991–99 I went to work as a staff artist for Neal Adams and his Continuity Studios, but the majority of the work done in their Burbank studio was not comic book related: we did storyboarding, animatics and concept art for TV, films, and commercials, as well as movie poster design. On occasion I was called upon to add some collaborative artwork to one of Continuity's comic book line, maybe some penciling or backgrounds.

With perhaps some irony, the genre that originally interested me in art—I was a voracious comic book reader from a very young age, and probably learned how to read from them—was never a major part of my professional work.

TDE: You mentioned your brother Paul's stories for *Mike Shayne*—the May and October 1980 issues. Did he write more or lose interest?

TG: Paul wrote a lot of stories and shopped them around, but those were the only two he ever successfully sold. I think he finally got discouraged; he might have continued to write, but he didn't try to submit the stories anymore. He did contribute a few humorous articles for one of his local newspapers.

After his passing in 2012, his kids found his "slush pile" of work and got together and self-published a nice collection of his stories and articles. It was a nice tribute. The cover art was done by my nephew Brendan Gleeson. My friend and colleague, author Terrill Lee Lankford, was nice

Mike Shayne Mystery Magazine October 1980 with Tony's cover and his brother Paul Gleeson's "Don't Touch That Dial!"

enough to provide a cover blurb.

TDE: You have a talented family. You've also done quite a bit of writing yourself. Tell us about it.

TG: There's a definite streak of creativity and a very warped sense of humor that has always abounded through my siblings and me and has been passed down to the subsequent generations.

As to my own writing: my first venture was in the early 1980s. I submitted an article to *Players Magazine* about a favorite musician, saxophonist Eric Dolphy, for whom I was doing a lot of illustration and had a cordial relationship with the editor, Emory Holmes. He was (understandably) a bit skeptical about an artist who fancied himself a writer but then he read the piece and liked it and ran it. He even tapped me to do an accompanying illustration. Thereafter, I sporadically wrote a handful of essays, criticism, and reviews, often about music, comics, or the business of illustration, for different periodicals. But I always wanted to try my hand at fiction, and in an extended format, and finally got my chance about ten years ago when a British publisher accepted my first crime novel for the Linford Mystery Series. They asked for more and I've now had nine titles published by them. Wildside Press here in the U.S. has repackaged and reissued several of them and will hopefully continue to do so. The books, I guess you'd call them procedurals, concern a police detective bureau called the Personal Crimes Unit which is based in a fictional (and unnamed) Western city. I was largely influenced by the narrative approach of Evan Hunter/ Ed McBain's great 87th Precinct series; he was a marvelous storyteller from whom an aspiring writer can learn a lot. Among other things, I've tried to shift the focus in the stories among a cast of leading characters and to try different story approaches to keep things from getting overly predictable. I'd also like to think I learned a few things from another favorite writer, Donald Westlake, in terms of keeping a plot interesting. Some of the books have a certain levity (or so I hope) while others are more serious. And the characters seem to have taken on their own lives to the point they now tell me what they're going to do.

Reference photo of Tony Gleeson and his granddaughter for the illustration at right.

I often get asked if I contributed anything graphic to the series, but I've found it more interesting to stay out of designing covers or doing interior illustration. I like being on the other side of the counter, so to speak, exploring another side of my psyche—and seeing what someone else does with those elements. So far they've been quite different from where I would have gone, and so far they've consistently and pleasantly surprised me. All in all I've got nine Linford titles and two Wildside "omnibus" editions, with a third scheduled to release early this year. I'm always happy to make a blatant, unashamed plug for them.

I've written a few stories that are more in the horror or science fiction vein but so far haven't had any luck in selling them. I did come up with some imagery to accompany those,

Frankenstein's monster menacing Jo March of *Little Women*.

so we'll see if that helps them get picked up. The game is still afoot.

TDE: Congratulations, Tony. What other recent projects have you done?

TG: In recent years I've done a lot of dinosaur and reptile related drawings, and a few years ago had an exhibition and a traveling show on that theme. Last year I participated in a crazy fun group show that was an art mashup of two books that celebrated significant anniversaries of publication: *Frankenstein* and *Little Women.* My contributions involved myself modeling as Frankenstein's Creature and my granddaughter posing as Jo March; it was as nuts and enjoyable as it sounds.

TDE: What advice do you have for aspiring artists?

TG: Duke Ellington famously said, "Don't give me inspiration, give me a deadline," and that sums up so much for me. You defeat blank paper syndrome by sitting down, and doing things until something works. You get inspiration not from some daemon or muse but from applying yourself, throwing stuff against the wall until something sticks. I've gone through reams of tracing paper on some jobs, just trying stuff until the right combination came along.

Deadlines can be beneficial because they force you to stop agonizing and second guessing, and to actually finish something.

Limitations present opportunities; sometimes restrictions bring you more freedom (a college English instructor once told me that there's only so much you can do standing in an empty field hitting a tennis ball, but put a set of lines around you and a set of rules and constraints, and suddenly you've got a whole world of possibilities of what you can do). They make you think in new ways. They should be embraced, not feared or dreaded.

And I've gotten to do a lot of cool stuff and encounter a lot of interesting people simply because I was willing to show up, show confidence that I could do something (whether or not I really could), and be willing to learn whatever I didn't know.

TDE: What's on your drawing board and/or typewriter

Self-portrait by Tony Gleeson for *The New Visions* a collection of cover artwork for the Science Fiction Book Club, Doubleday, 1981

as of February 2020?

TG: I'm currently working on a new Personal Crimes novel to be submitted to Wildside by the end of the year. And they are releasing a new omnibus of two of my books, *Jessica's Death* and *Sometimes They Die*, in the next month or two.

And . . . currently finishing up one of my favorite annual projects, generating all the graphics for the Vintage Paperback Collectors' Show in Glendale (CA), which happens this year on March 8. For over a dozen years now I've created their posters, fliers, and all the other promotional material, as well as their signage and anything else that involves imagery. Plus, I'm always at the show, which is great fun.

There's also a sketchbook project emerging from the back burner: for the past few years I've been working in a series of sketchbooks, stream-of-conscious doodles to keep my wrist loose and my drawing facility up. There are a lot of dinosaurs and reptiles involved (as mentioned above, a lot of my recent work has gone that route) and I've got hundreds of pieces from which to hopefully cull out a book if all goes well.

I'm also hoping to do more team-up appearances in coming months with my longtime friend and colleague, Odie Hawkins, where we talk about our individual books and our collaborations (Odie is the author of something like 40 books and I've illustrated numerous of his books and articles). We did several appearances last year at bookshops in the Los Angeles area, having a rollicking good time, two extremely disparate creators riffing on our work and our experiences, interviewed/moderated (or per-

haps kept from overly digressing is a better term) with grace and humor by Zola Selena Hawkins. And of course, we always have our books available for anyone interested in picking one or more up.

And who knows what else will come calling any time on my phone or email?

TDE: What's the best way for readers to stay current with your projects?

TG: I seem to have the best response on social media, specifically from my Facebook pages. There's a public page called "Tony Gleeson, Illustrator," and I also post a number of public albums from my personal page (my icon is a were-wolf). I've noticed a considerable uptick in attention and recognition at shows and such since I started those up, so that's where I devote the most attention to promotion.

I've also started a writer's blog on the Goodreads site to talk about the literary side of things.

Linford Mysteries by Tony Gleeson

- Night Music Nov. 2015
- It's Her Fault May 2016
- A Question of Guilt July 2016
- The Other Frank Jan. 2017
- Jessica's Death April 2017
- Sometimes They Die Feb. 2018
- The Pieman's Last Song Oct. 2018
- The Last Step Nov. 2019
- Find the Money Jan. 2020

Personal Crimes Mystery Series Wildside Press

- No. 1 Night Music; Open and Shut
- No. 2 It's Her Fault; The Other Frank
- No. 3 Jessica's Death; Sometimes They Die

El Despoblado

Fiction by Michael Bracken
Illustration by Rick McCollum

"The first DQ restaurant was located in Joliet, Illinois. It was operated by Sherb Noble and opened for buiness on June 22, 1940. It served a variety of frozen products, such as soft serve ice cream."
–Wikipedia

When the Dairy Queen closes, a town is finished, and Earl Stovall was doing his personal best to see that didn't happen, stopping in every afternoon for a large dip cone.

"It ain't enough," Jeremiah Hervy told him.

Earl was the only customer in the place and the two men repeated a conversation they'd had too many times before.

"I haven't taken a paycheck in months," Jeremiah continued. In many Texas communities, Dairy Queen was the first fast food franchise to open. In dying communities, it was often the last to close. So, Jeremiah had been cooking the books to make the franchise appear more successful than it was, but he said he couldn't do it much longer. "There just isn't enough traffic."

They both glanced out the window at the state highway bisecting their town. The only thing moving was Emma Marchant, who shifted her walker a fraction of an inch at a time as she made her way home from the antiques store where she sold—on the rare occasion she sold anything at all—items she had scavenged from Flytrap's abandoned homes and businesses.

Seeing her, Earl said, "If Emma doesn't feed soon, we're going to lose her."

Jeremiah nodded his assent.

After he finished his dip cone, Earl returned to The Lone Star Inn, a six-room motel at the edge of town he had purchased from the previous owner several decades earlier. Having not hosted an overnight guest in weeks, he was surprised to see a large, broad-shouldered man standing in the office, slapping the counter bell repeatedly with the flat of his hand.

Earl entered behind him. "May I help you?"

The man spun around. "Where the hell have you been? I've been ringing this damned bell forever."

"I'm sorry," Earl said as he moved behind the counter. "I'm here now. How can I help you?"

The man paid cash to rent the room at the far end of the building. Earl watched as he moved his car where it could not be seen from the street, then removed a suitcase and a duffel bag from the trunk and carried them into Room Six.

Once the man closed the door, Earl stepped into his apartment behind the office and switched on his surveillance equipment, equipment so old it still required videocassette tapes to record whatever images the room cameras captured. Then he phoned the Dairy Queen. When Jeremiah answered, he said, "We've got a live one, and he's hiding something. He registered as John Smith."

Sixteenth-century Spanish explorers had named the Big Bend area of Texas *el despoblado*—the uninhabited—and Flytrap, a never-thriving community that grew up around a freshwater spring, that had once served weary travelers on their way to or from northern Mexico. During the first hundred years of the town's existence, Earl and Jeremiah and Emma and others like them had drifted into Flytrap from around the world. Jeremiah had opened his Dairy Queen in the late 1940s when the town was still hopeful and the chain was growing at a rapid pace. More travelers stopped in Flytrap to visit the DQ than for any other reason, but it wasn't enough to prevent the slow decline of the town.

When Earl saw his motel's lone guest exit his room, he stepped into the front office. He stood waiting when Mr. Smith pushed the door open and asked, "Where can a guy get something to eat in this town?"

Earl pointed him toward the Dairy Queen. "It's the only place."

He called Jeremiah to tell him Mr. Smith was on his way and added, "Call me in Six when he leaves."

Earl let himself into Room Six and examined the man's luggage, finding a box of 9mm shells in the suitcase and the duffel bag filled with cash. He was closing the duffel bag when the phone rang twice.

He ducked out of the room, hurried back to the office, and was behind the counter when Mr. Smith walked past carrying a takeout bag in one hand and a Blizzard in the other. Then he watched on the monitor as Mr. Smith entered his room, settled on the bed, and ate his dinner while flipping channels on the television. He finally settled on the evening news.

"And in other news," the male anchor said, "a pair of gunmen robbed a check cashing store in Amarillo earlier today, making off with more than half a million dollars in cash. Shots were exchanged between the robbers and the store's owner. Several hours later the body of a man believed to be one of the robbers was found along the highway outside Midland. Police believe the pair was headed toward Mexico when the dead man succumbed to his gunshot wounds and was abandoned by his partner."

Mr. Smith switched the channel until he found a rerun of *Big Bang Theory* on the only other station with a signal strong enough to reach Flytrap. He finished his dinner as the sitcom played out and then cleaned up the mess.

Earl was still watching his guest a few hours later when Jeremiah closed the Dairy Queen and walked down the street to join him. They had spent many nights together watching motel guests—from adventurous young couples performing sexual acrobatics to dysfunctional families who had taken wrong turns in their search for Big Bend National Park—and they always waited until certain it was safe to take them.

They were wrong about Mr. Smith. They entered his room to find Mr. Smith sitting on the side of the bed with a semi-automatic pistol pointed at them.

"You after the money or the reward?"

Jeremiah glanced at Earl, wondering what he was missing.

"Neither," Earl said.

"Then what the hell are you doing in my room?"

"We came for you."

Mr. Smith squeezed the trigger three times before the old men were upon him, and he never knew if he actually shot either of them.

Earl and Jeremiah used a wheelbarrow to transport Mr. Smith's body to Emma Marchant's front porch. She needed it more than they did, and they would split the next meal delivered by providence. They rang her doorbell bell and returned to the motel before she even answered.

As they cleaned Room Six, Earl showed Jeremiah the duffel bag filled with money, letting him know they had killed two birds with one stone. Then they disposed of Mr. Smith's car thirty miles away in the Rio Grande, where it joined several others they had disposed of over the years.

The next morning, Emma Marchant jogged across the state highway from her home to the Dairy Queen where Earl and Jeremiah were having breakfast. No longer emaciated, she had no need to use the walker.

"That was quite a treat you left me last night, boys," she said. With a lascivious wink, she added. "Why don't you two come over tonight and I'll treat you to a little something you haven't had in quite some time."

Michael Bracken is the coeditor of *Black Cat Mystery Magazine* and editor of the anthology *The Eyes of Texas* (Down & Out Books).

"I did my research on human teenagers. Apparently, they communicate mostly through shrugs and eyerolls."

Lake County Incidents
By Alec Cizak

Review by Richard Krauss

Alec Cizak is a writer and filmmaker, originally from Indiana, where all the stories in this collection take place. His novels include *Down on the Street* and *Breaking Glass*. He's also the editor of the fiction journal *Pulp Modern* a joint production of Uncle B Publications and Larque Press.

Creepy (originally from BeatToAPulp.com 2017)

Neighborhood cronies in Lublin, Indiana seem to have a serial killer on their hands. Nobody they know would violate the young female victims before and after slitting their throats like that, so common sense leads them to the stranger's van with Missouri plates parked in the Walmart lot for the better part of a month.

The cherry on the top of this creepy cruller is the pithy narration:

"Several nights of debate led to the obvious conclusion that the Turkey Creek Killer, as the Free Press *had taken to calling him, her, or it, could not be someone local. We were church-going folk. Most of us were Lutheran. A few were Catholics, but we forgave them. Politically, we leaned toward the right, though there were a good number of liberals amongst us who, as predicted, suggested we not rush to judgment."*

Cancers

A ghostly image splayed across window panes haunts Danuta when she returns to Haggard for her mother's funeral. She hasn't looked back for twenty-five years since she left for California, or seen her younger sister, Kristyna, who never left their hometown.

The night before the funeral, Danuta stays in her mom's old house, recalling regrets of past abuses—as victim and offender—as a powerful midwestern thunderstorm knocks out her power and big-city bravado, the mysterious spirit triggering her comeuppance.

Atomic Fuel
(*The Digest Enthusiast* No. 6)

Claims Adjuster for Agra Insurance, Sal Bridgewater, hears an infectious jingle for an energy drink on his way to work. What the hell?

He tries it not ten minutes later. One drink of Atomic Fuel and Sal's a whole new misfit. The action breezes along in a logical transgression while our narrator skewers a day in the life of the United Corporations of America. The two key actors in this humorous jaunt, Sal, the victim,

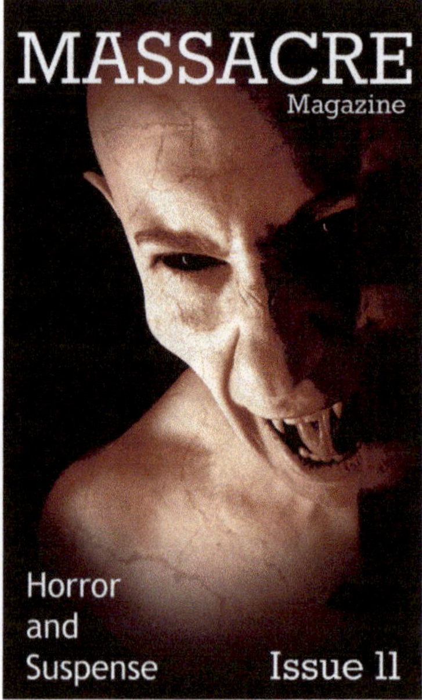

and his best new beverage, the incident. Everybody else, however finely painted, boil down to their roles. Like an artificial 8-ounce shot of vigor it's quick and refreshing, and then it's over—you decide where things regress from here.

Sidewalk Flowers

(MicroHorror.com 2018)

Helen Bobble is pushing 80. Every day she's out-of-doors watering the sidewalk out front like a sad habit. The neighborhood kids think she's bonkers, and they don't mind poking some fun. What's the harm, long as nobody gets hurt? With only two pages to tell her side, Helen loses no time sharing her sidewalk secret with one of her biggest pests.

Canopy Road

If you heard the sound of trouble would you heed its warning, or would you, like most, require visual confirmation of the threat you would so much rather deny? There is menace in the air above Canopy Road. More precisely, in the treetops above. But let's put that aside. To begin, there's a softer edge to the telling of this tale that reflects the three middle-class boys at its center, as hints of the grown-up world begin to intrude on their pop culture milieu of the Midwest in the early '80s.

There are two threats to their existence. One is unknown, vicious, and eminent. The other may more insidious, because it's part of them. Their fathers' stubborn, unwavering righteousness of certainty. The denial of change, evolution, and facts. Can anyone survive such abject ambiguity unscathed?

Emuq (*Massacre Magazine* No. 11)

A macabre tale of temptation and desire that reads like a classic horror story planted in the modern world. A bookshop clerk's stilted self-awareness melds with his obsession for his lovely boss, leading him to the forbidden Emuq volume.

What motivates such grim determination? Is it possible to judge one's motivations purely?

"You must employ this gift in the service of others, not yourself. This is the mistake many men have made over the centuries. Should you use it, in any way, for your own benefit, those same demons will return and drag you to oblivion and drain your blood to ink the next edition of Emuq set loose upon the Earth."

Once read, there is no healing reversal of the book's deadly promise.

Stuck (*Horror Bites Magazine* No. 6)

"If you go to the highway, you can see where Mr. Shipwick's wife's car got smashed by that semi. Or you can take State Road 53 into town and see Donny Gross get run over by that bull, over there at the Franklin farm, you remember that?"

History writes the future. Outsider Jessica talks her friend Emily into things. Ghost is a new drug that enables visions of . . . well, ghosts. Now that Jessica's done it, it's Emily's turn. Who wouldn't want to revisit loved ones lost to us forever? But there's a catch or two that turns poor Emily's trip from reunion to incident. Great characters and premise make this ghoulish tale unsettling and poignant.

The Bridge

A divorced mom forces her teenage daughter and her younger sister to move in with Dad while she finds herself in Morocco. The youngster is a perfect angel, the teen rarely civil. Desperate to

connect with his older daughter, Dad agrees to chase down a ghost story with her, hoping to bond.

"You park your car at the edge of the ravine. Just after four in the morning, a woman opens the back door and gets in behind you."

Magic may ensue, don't look back. A satisfying ghost story laced with conditions designed to snag.

Broke

They'd met at a bank. "He'd walked straight up and said he wanted to chill with her. No games. No bullshit. He didn't talk law shop, he didn't speak the liberal arts gibberish she'd been indoctrinated with as an undergrad at Ohio State." Someday, she imagined they'd have kids.

Her salary far exceeds his, so when she's fired they pack up everything and move into a cheaper place.

The first night, exhausted from the move, she just wants to get to bed. Then she notices the window

the porch of their vacation cabin, her shriek brings her husband on a run. Her overreaction triggers a giddy response. He holds the thing up to show Carrie it's harmless. She slaps his hand away, tearing the slimy thing loose.

"The worm somersaulted through the air, arced toward her husband. She expected him to move, but he stayed still, his jaw dropped wide open. The worm flew into his mouth. He grabbed his throat and coughed."

Somehow he keeps the disgusting swallow down, and after a profuse apology from his wife, they attempt to get on with their day. Unfortunately, Ben's tummy doesn't feel very well, and that's just the start of their troubles.

The People in the Margins

College student Kayla Pugh has issues with her parents, her self-image, her school—seemingly every single thing.

"She didn't have panic attacks often. Any time she felt one coming on, she looked on her phone or her computer for something to be offended by and that would distract her long enough to wiggle out of her own head."

She's savvy enough to employ ad-blockers, but somehow one pops up beside her twitter feed. One she can't ignore. A free download of the ebook *The Complete History of the People in the Margins*. It strikes a chord. She is a person in the margins for Chrissake.

"As she scanned the text, it became clear the book had nothing to do with marginalized populations. Something about a cult in nearby Pawpaw Grove.

in the bathroom. It's late, but there's sunlight streaming in from outside. All the other room's windows are dark as they should be.

After her husband investigates, he's different, like a man obsessed.

Useful Things

(*EconoClash Review* No. 2)

A dumpster dive at the behest of Gideon's fiancé yields a smear of orange gel across his palm. Back home, he scrubs the goo off, but the inciting damage has taken root.

There's something extra creepy about medical horror stories. You know they're not real, but they seem more plausible than many horror motifs.

Worms

(*Indiana Horror Review* 2015)

If there's one thing that scares Carrie, it's worms. When she spots a big black one in the study by

A group of early Indiana settlers who were not Protestants."

The locals shunned these outsiders, eventually branding them witches and dubbed them The People in the Margins. When their entire group is found hung together in a grove of Sycamores, The Lublin Free Press ran the official story—Mass Suicide.

But their legacy left haunting reminders of their extermination, and Kayla seems particularly receptive.

Summary

Lake County Incidents is a satisfying collection of macabre stories with engaging hooks, authentic characters, and masterful prose. Highly recommended for students of the unusual.

Lake County Incidents by Alex Cizak
ABC Group Documentation, 2019
5.5" x 8.5" 142 pages
Print $11.99 Kindle $2.99

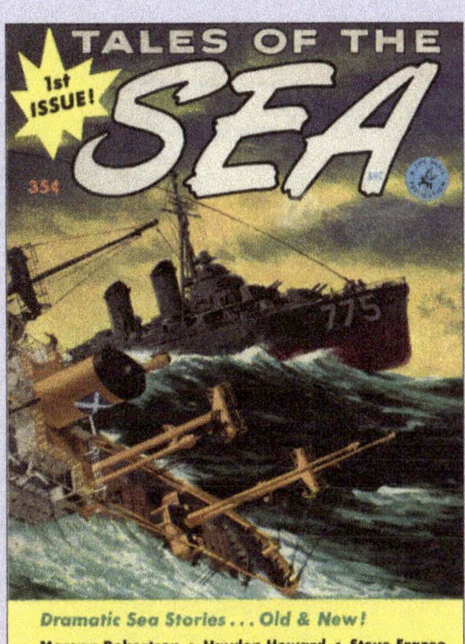

Tales of the Sea

Ziff-Davis Publishing Company, Chicago, IL
Published Quarterly
One issue
Vol. 1 No. 1 Spring 1953
Editor: Howard Browne
Managing Editor: L.E. Shaffer
Associate Editor: Paul W. Fairman
Art Editor: L.R. Summers
Wrap-around cover by Clarence Doore.
5.5" x 7.75"
148 pages (including covers)
35¢ cover price

Contents

"The Fourth Man" by John Russell
"The Enemies" by Morgan Robertson
"Are You a Weekend Sailor?" by John Weston
"The Terrible Solomons" by Jack London
"Down Among the Rock Cod"
   by Hayden Howard
"The Skipper and El Captain"
   by Frank R. Stockton
"Without Orders" by William E. Vance
"The Unsinkable Ship that Sank"
   by Karl Baarslag
"The Crew of the Foraker" by Steve Frazee
"The Gentleman from San Francisco"
   by Ivan Bunin

Lester del Rey's

The Five Ages of Science Fiction

Article by Ward Smith

A reflection upon the topic I wrote about in *The Digest Enthusiast* No. 11 i.e., the format change to digest-size by *Astounding Science Fiction* in 1944. This piece concerns the "comings and goings" of the science fiction digest magazines.
–Ward Smith

Science fiction writer and editor Lester del Rey (1915–1993) also became a historian of sorts regarding the subject of science fiction writing and publishing. That was best illustrated in his *The World of Science Fiction, 1926–1976—The History of a Subculture*, (New York, Del Rey Books, 1979).

In that work he described what he called "The Five Ages of Science Fiction." Del Rey's speculations are very interesting, although they may be open to a lot of discussion. The age-segments were:

1. The Age of Wonder— 1926–1937 Hugo Gernsback and the legacy of the specialty science fiction magazine.

2. The Golden Age— 1938–1949 John W. Campbell Jr., *Astounding*, and world conventions devoted to science fiction.

3. The Age of Acceptance— 1950–1961 The *Galaxy Science Fiction* magazine years, the great magazine newsstand glut, and science-fiction fandom unfettered.

4. The Age of Rebellion— 1962–1973 Sex, Harlan Ellison, the New Wave, *Star Trek* on TV, and science fiction accepted in the schools at last.

5. The Fifth Age—1974 Science fiction hits the big time in the media, *Star Wars* and after, and a convention every week.

I have summarized del Rey's five

Unknown Nov. 1939. Cover by Graves Gladney.

"ages" but suggest adding one more:

6. The Age of Swords, Sorcery and Sagas—1980s–Present

Marked by the predominance of magic and fantasy, the decline of hard science in "science fiction," the liberalizing of the term science fiction to be replaced by "speculative fiction," and the rise of multi-volume sagas that go on ad infinitum both in

Astounding Science Fiction Sept. 1949.
Cover by Paul Orban.

Fantastic Adventures Dec. 1950.
Cover by Robert Gibson Jones.

book form and in the visual media [TV, movies]. In other words: Science Fiction became big business!

Survivor—Science Fiction Style

As of 1930 we had: *Amazing Stories, Astounding Stories, Wonder Stories,* and *Weird Tales.* These were the sustaining and sustainable fantasy and science fiction publications of that time. Many others came and went. There was a spate of "startups" as the 1930s closed viz. *Famous Fantastic Mysteries, Planet Stories, Startling Stories,* and the lost, lamented *Unknown Worlds.* The Gernsback-founded *Wonder Stories* continued under the new title *Thrilling Wonder Stories.*

The Wartime Survivors According to Ashley

By the Winter of 1945–46 only six SF magazines in America survived, according to Ashley. (Michael Ashley, *The History of the Science Fiction Magazine*, Vol. 3, Chicago, Henry Regenery, 1977)

Amazing Stories (now with juvenile slant, sensationalism)

Astounding Science-Fiction (sophisticated, scientific; by mid-1945 it was the only digest)

Famous Fantastic Mysteries (classic reprints) + *Fantastic Novels* (on and off)

Planet Stories (space opera, mostly with a juvenile slant)

Startling Stories (adventure, action; generally juvenile slant)

Thrilling Wonder Stories (*Astounding*'s rival with steadily improving quality of SF stories)

But Ashley left out: The entire conglomerate of Columbia Publications' "just-get-along science fiction magazines," *Future Science Fiction,* (The original) *Science Fiction Stories,* and *Science Fiction Quarterly. Science Fiction Stories* turned into a digest, on-and-off, in the mid-1950s. *Science Fiction Quarterly* became famous for being the last pulp-size and style SF magazine.

Ashley also overlooked *Fantastic Adventures* which was Ziff-Davis/Ray Palmer's "borderline science fiction" with a sensationalistic juvenile slant. He also did not include *Weird Tales* which was also borderline with its emphasis on horror, mystery and fantasy, and only some science fiction.

The Digest–War Survivors

My observation of the state of science fiction magazines by the end of 1960 is this:

Amazing Stories (Revived in 2018 by Experimenter Publishing as a full size magazine.)

Astounding/Analog Science Fact/Fiction (now just *Analog Science Fiction*)

Fantastic (which changed names regularly, and later merged with *Amazing*)

Galaxy Science Fiction (had once been *Astounding*'s principal rival)

IF (or) *Worlds of IF Science Fiction* (struggled, then later absorbed by *Galaxy*)

The Magazine of Fantasy & Science Fiction or *F&SF* (a class act, durable)

. . . and the ragged-edged pulps were now as extinct as the brontosaurus!

As the 20th-century was ending, only *Analog* and *F&SF* remained from the above half-dozen survivors, joined by *Isaac Asimov's Science Fiction Magazine*, which had made it through from the 1970s, defying the odds.

Amazing was revived in 1998 for 10 quarterly, large, slick issues. *Weird Tales* also returned from the magazine graveyard the same

Fantasy & Science Fiction Dec. 1958. Cover by Ed Emshwiller.

year as a quarterly. (The lastest revival under Editor Marvin Kaye is No. 363 in ~2019.)

Survivors' Statistics in the 21st Century:

I went online to check on the status of current fantasy and science fiction magazines and found the following for the beginning of the year 2010 (Compare this list to the "biggies" of 1930, above.):

Analog Science Fiction and Fact
Asimov's Science Fiction
The Magazine of Fantasy and Science Fiction

Within the span from about 1960 to just past the turn into the 21st century, there were various ventures such as *Cemetery Dance*, Marion Zimmer Bradley's Fantasy Magazine, *Absolute Magnitude*, *Aboriginal Science Fiction*, *Worlds of Fantasy and Horror*, and of course *Omni* (1978–1995) which tried to bridge the gap from science to sci-

Analog Science Fiction and Fact Oct. 2008.
Cover by Scott Grimando.

Stellar 7 Science Fiction Stories Oct. 2008.
Cover by David B. Mattingly.

ence fiction, just as Hugo Gernsback had attempted with his *Electrical Experimenter* and *Science & Invention*. What goes around comes around; or is it what comes around.

Space prohibits trying to name the numerous short-lived and one-shot titles. These sprang up like weeds among the science-fiction publishing garden fruits.

The Paperback Rebellion

A new breed of "periodical" emerged from the chaos of the digests and the dust of the pulps. That is, the paperback book qua periodical series of stories, or "Paperback Magazine." These were not anthologies nor annual "Best Stories of…" publications but collections of new writings in hardcover (HC) or paperback (PB) format. By the mid-1960s these began to supplant SF magazines, just as digests had pushed the pulps off the market.

There was a series of seven books edited by Judy-Lynn del Rey starting in 1974 called *Stellar*, including one additional volume entitled *Stellar Short Novels*. Fan-turned-pro Terry Carr edited the *Universe* series of seven or so HC volumes.

Roger Elwood edited *Continuum*, a series of original stories in PB from Berkley-Medallion from 1973 to 1975, four volumes in all. And from about 1970 there was *Infinity* edited by Robert Hoskins. There was a series entitled *Destinies*, subtitled "The Paperback Magazine of Science Fiction & Speculative Fact" from Ace Books. There were the "Best of—" reprint volumes edited by Judith Merril.

Another "new" was Robert Silverberg's *New Dimensions*, which appeared in three volumes from 1971 to 1974. There also appeared *Quark* in 1970–71, and a solo issue of *SF Emphasis* in 1974. Berkley-Medallion published four or five volumes of a series called *Orbit* (not the magazine), under the capable editorship of Damon Knight, April 1966 to December 1968.

There are (were) also the DAW books named for Donald A. Wollheim at Ace Publications. Some of those were collections, just as Wollheim had pioneered the original-story publication with his 1949 *The Girl With the Hungry Eyes*.

But the outstanding example of the PB (or HC) "periodical" is Ballantine's *Star Science Fiction* series, edited by Frederik Pohl. These appeared from early 1953 to ca. January 1960. (When Pohl left to edit *Galaxy*, this series died.) All stories were original. Authors were well known and the quality of material was very good, some of it even being anthologized in turn.

Now, these are gone as well.

Ward Smith is a pen name used by a collector of vintage books with paper wraps, including Armed Services Editions, original Pocket Books, Dell "Mapbacks," and some early wartime digests.

The Book of Wit & Humor
Mercury Books, Inc. New York, NY
Volume One 1953
Cover and cartoons: Saul Steinberg
Publisher: Lawrence E. Spivak
Editor: Louis Untermeyer
General Manager: Joseph W. Ferman
Managing Editor: Charles Angoff
Art Director: George Salter
Assistant Editor: Judith R. Spivak
5.5" x 7.75"
128 pages
35¢ cover price

Captain Future in Love
by Allen Steele

Review by Richard Krauss

"Swashbuckling action, perilous adventure, and a lady to die for . . . all in the return of a space legend!".
–Back cover blurb, *Captain Future in Love* Experimenter Publishing, 2019

Those who subscribe to the latest iteration of *Amazing Stories* are already familiar with this story, as it was first serialized in the first and second issues. But this consolidation is loaded with bonus material, and its digest-size delivers a very pleasing package.

Amazing Selects is the beginning of a new series of novella-length stories published by Steve Davidson and the Experimenter Publishing Company LLC. Behind its cover by Tony Sart, the book opens with a series of short introductions by its Editors and Publisher. It's followed by a three-page backgrounder on the major characters of the Captain Future series, and a two-page spread of technical art of the Futuremen's spacecraft, the Comet and Comet II, rendered by Rob Casell, who also provides over half a dozen illustrations throughout the novella.

The follow-on to Steele's *Avengers of the Moon* (Tor, 2017), *Captain Future in Love* is the first part of *The Return of Ul Quorn*, and launches the next adventure, *The Guns of Pluto*. The series will continue with two additional novellas making up the final book of a trilogy *The Horror at Jupiter*.

Like the Tor novel, this one provides a much-needed modernization of the cast, a thrilling space adventure that's part of a larger story arc, and a chance to enjoy a new outing with one of the greatest heroes from the golden age of pulp.

The prologue of *The Return of Ul Quorn* opens on New Year's Eve 2304 aboard the *Titan King*, luxury cruiser, on a "Journey to the Rings." While its passengers enjoy the ballet and orchestra in the spaceliner's swank observation dome, its captain responds to a distress call from a shuttlecraft, one *Skylark*, outbound from Mimas on its way to Iapetus.

Despite reservations, since a rendezvous will ruin the timing of their flight through the Encke Gap of the A Ring, Saturn's outermost ring, Captain Lamont yields to protocol and prepares the *Titan King* to dock with the shuttle.

Once aboard the *King*, Lamont learns the *Skylark*'s ruse. The shuttle is under the command of the Black Pirate and his crew. "Baseline *Homo sapiens* from Earth mainly, but

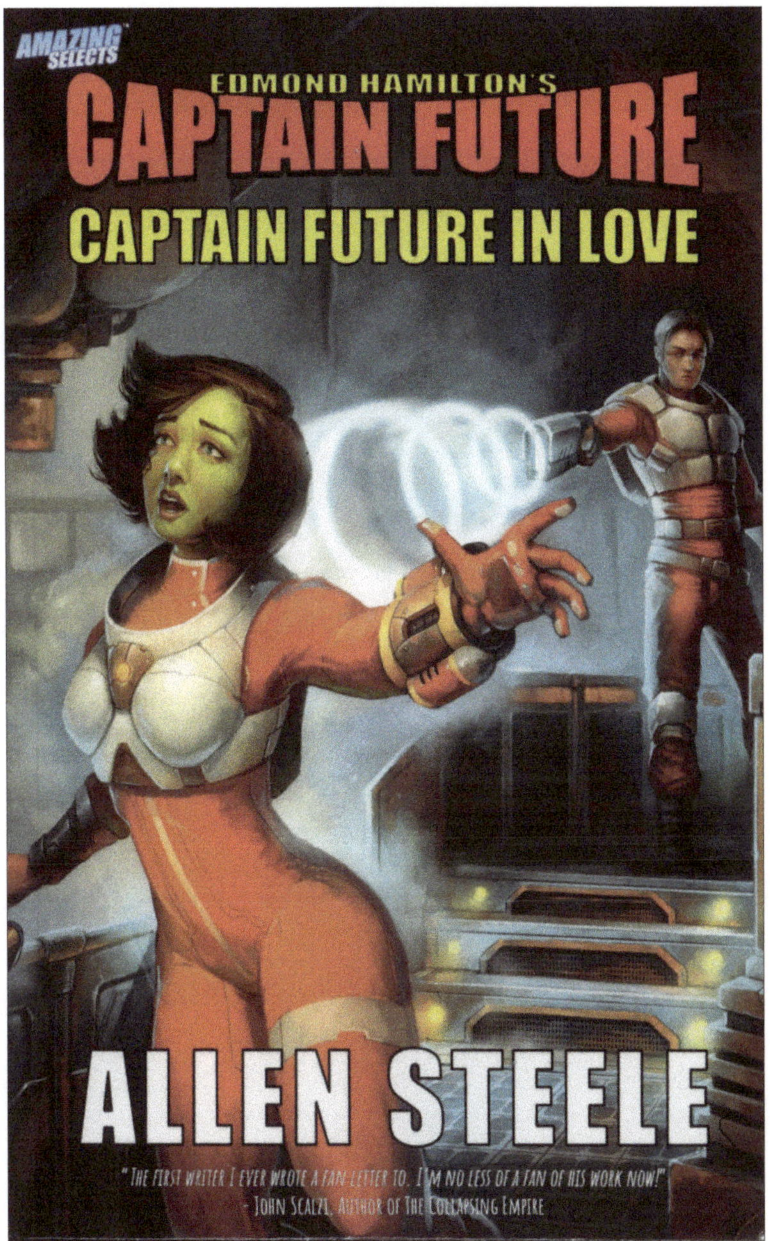

also a few *Homo cosmos*: two more aresians, both men; an aphrodite, ebony-skinned, hairless, and thin; a massive, hirsute jovian who looked as if he could bend Hari al-Sarakka [the *King*'s helmsman] like a pretzel. They were genetically-altered cousins of the human race, their ancestors genengineered to inhabit other worlds of the solar

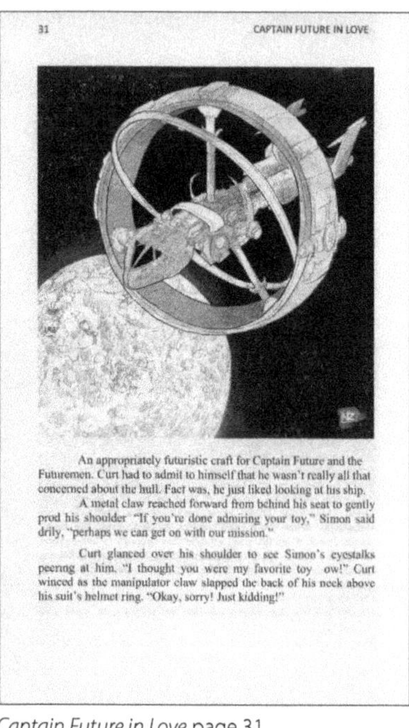

An appropriately futuristic craft for Captain Future and the Futuremen. Curt had to admit to himself that he wasn't really all that concerned about the hull. Fact was, he just liked looking at his ship.

A metal claw reached forward from behind his seat to gently prod his shoulder "If you're done admiring your toy," Simon said drily, "perhaps we can get on with our mission."

Curt glanced over his shoulder to see Simon's eyestalks peering at him. "I thought you were my favorite toy   ow!" Curt winced as the manipulator claw slapped the back of his neck above his suit's helmet ring. "Okay, sorry! Just kidding!"

Captain Future in Love page 31
Comet II by Rob Caswell

system, fundamentally human yet alien at the same time."

The Black Pirate and his band seize control of the *King*'s crew and order the evacuation of all passengers and non-critical support crew. He reveals his allegiance to Starry Messenger…"the inter-planetary separatist group—a self-described 'liberation movement'—dedicated to wresting control of Mars, the major asteroids and Galilean moons, and other inhabited worlds of the outer solar system from the Solar Coalition."

To what end does the hijacking of the *Titan King* lead? Patience—with the prologue's events set in motion, part one of *The Return of Ul Quorn*, *Captain Future in Love*, begins—about three months later. Curt Newton and the Futuremen secretly board the massive Venera Stratos, a colony and refining plant in permanent orbit above the uninhabitible planet Venus. They fear the station may have been infiltrated by Starry Messenger, hence their stealthy arrival. Curt is the first to arrive and his mind drifts back to his first visit to *Venera Stratos* as a teenager.

The trip was part of his education, learning to assimilate other people and cultures after a childhood spent in seclusion on Earth's Moon with only the pseudo-human companionship of Dr. Simon Wright, aka the Brain, the android, Otho, and Grag, a sentient robot. Simon has scheduled a non-stop itinerary of aphrodite museums and tours, fast-tracking local culture and assigning tutorials every night for Curt to study in the comfort of his hotel room. But Curt was coming of age and rebellious of Simon's constant lecturing and control.

By the second day, Curt has had enough. On a break, off campus from the Tsiolkovsky University, he and Otho sit on the rounded edge of an ornate fountain. An aphrodite girl about Curt's age catches his eye. When he and Otho begin to argue, the girl intuits his resistance to authority and gives him a wink—just the encouragement he needs.

That night, she returns and quietly lures him away from the Venera Hotel and his companions, into the dark, Venusian night. Her name is Ashi, and she lives on the borders of aphrodite society.

Her story is slowly revealed to Curt over a series of nights and days as she shows him another side of life on *Venera Stratos*, while their feelings for each other grow.

Her mother and father were a mixed race couple—human and

aphrodite—shunned by purists who thought of themselves as the most advanced branch of humanity's tree. "Yet, when her parents finally made the decision to immigrate to Earth, she decided to remain."

She is an outlaw, stealing from the wealthy to sustain her existence. Swept up in her charms and independence, Curt ignores the moral conflicts her lifestyle inflames.

Back in the present, more trouble is brewing on *Venera Stratos*. There will be momentary resolution, but the larger threat of Starry Messenger is far from over, which the one-page preview of the next story makes perfectly clear.

The novella is followed by a personal history of author Allen Steele's introduction to the Futuremen and the path that led him to continue the series.

The volume closes with short bios of the author, interior artist Rob Caswell, and cover artist Tony Sart.

Tor missed an opportunity to complete the trilogy that began with *Avengers of the Moon*. Fortunately, for fans of the Futuremen *Amazing Selects* is here to insure the epic story is told.

Amazing Selects
Captain Future in Love (*The Return of Ul Quorn*, Book I) by Allen Steele
5.5" x 8.5" 130 pages
Print and Kindle $6.99 each

Your source for Adventure House, Steeger Books, Stark House Press & Other Fine Pulp-Related Books & Periodicals

REGULAR CATALOG ISSUED

mikechomko@gmail.com
https://sites.google.com/site/mikechomkobooks/

Fotocrime

Article by Richard Krauss

"Fotocrime is looking for factual material on true-crime subjects which should be brought to the attention of the American public."
–From the indicia of *Fotocrime* Vol. 1 No. 1

The unique phenomenon of pocket-size (4" x 6") magazines propagated newsstands in the 1950s. Most filled their pages with pin-ups of models, aspiring actresses, and stars of burlesque. Only a handful were dedicated to true crime stories, like *Fotocrime*.

The brainchild of editor and publisher Jackson Burke, *Fotocrime* sought the sensational horrors of butchers, mobsters, and serial killers; amping up fears of thrill-killing juvies and a continually degenerating society. Judging from its salacious covers, Burke targeted male readers as did most of *Fotocrime*'s advertisements for home movies, Texas homesites, surplus tools, rupture girdles, illustrated comic booklets (the kind men like), storm windows, quick-fix auto and TV gadgets, itch creams, and correspondence courses in crime detection, radio repair, and mathematics.

Ad rep D. Geller must've had his hands full. Ad turnover allowed plenty of space for a new batch of suckers every issue. So much for the power of repetition.

The indicia claimed a monthly schedule, but *Fotocrime* appeared sporadically over its four-issue run from December 1954 thru May 1955. Each issue ran 68 pages (counting covers) and sold for 15¢. Interior pages were black-and-white on newsprint, while the covers were three-color, until the final issue went full color— all printed on glossy stock.

The original masthead of outlined letters was replaced with a bolder design on the last issue, although the new look didn't carry through to the contents page which retained the original outline treatment. Inside, the basic layout emphasized photography with only a quarter to half a page of text on each page. Often the photos filled theentire page with white blocks for text laid on top. Photo captions like "rite" instead of "right" conjure memories of Forrest J Ackerman's *Famous Monsters of Filmland*.

The contents of *Fotocrime* contained 7- to 5-page feature stories and shorter, repeating departments: **Crime Camera** captured an

Fotocrime No. 1 December 1954.

incriminating snapshot like that of the elderly man with his fingers in the cash register of a supply company somewhere in Houston, Texas (No. 1). His arrest was left to readers' imaginations. Issue No. 2 presents a two-page fuzzy photograph of officer Eugene F. Simmons clinging to a telephone pole while holding a burglary suspect on the roof of the store he'd just robbed, at gun point. Issue No. 3 offers a cluster of unrelated images—most striking a young woman begging her dead fiancé to "Come back!" after a "playful scuffle" in which he received a

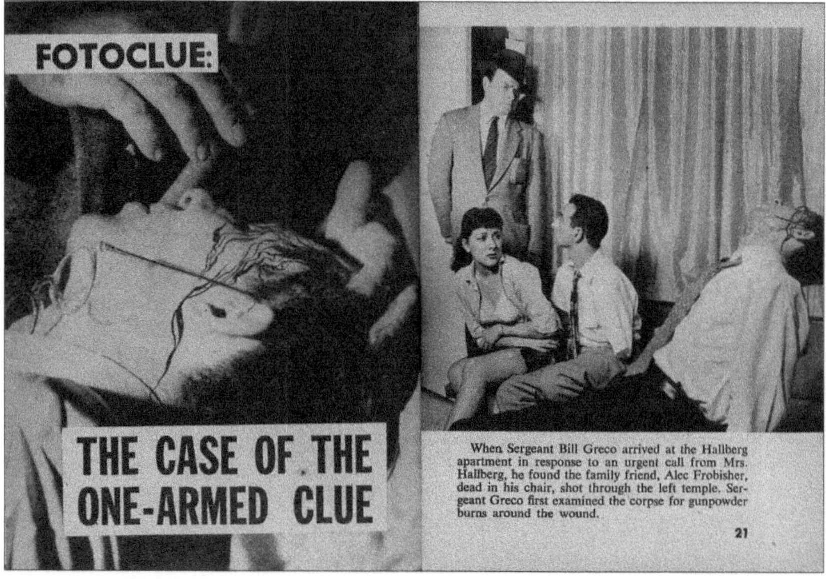

The opening spread of the Fotoclue department from *Fotocrime* No. 3 March 1955. These reenactment photos show the typical blood spatter technique used by the magazine's photographer.

fatal knife wound to the neck! Issue No. 4 shows bank robber Gehrhardt W. Puff in a gun fight with the Feds and the body of TV actor Sanford Tillis, bound with cord among the ashes of the fire his killer set to cover up the murder. (It didn't work.)

Gangland Grapevine features crime scene carnage of gangland shootings. The first, inside the Trap Door Club on New York's lower east side (No. 1), George Pare, booked on a hit-run killing (No. 2), gangland victims Tony Brancato, Tony Trombino, and "Buck" Emmino (No. 4), and Martin Accardo (No. 3), reflecting on his arrested for tax fraud, "Ever since they nailed Capone on a tax rap, they been gettin' after us guys. They can't pin nothin' on yuh, so they get yuh for taxes. It just ain't fair!"

Foto-clue features the reenactment of a crime with models posing for the real-life victims and perps.

The cases are so contrived, it's hard to believe they were authentic. In each outing an investigator reviews the clues, then challenges readers to solve the mystery, revealed on the final page. Inspector Maclean handles the first two cases (No. 1 & 2) and Sergeant Bill Greco the final two (No. 3 & 4). All are domestic squabbles that end in murder, leaving Maclean or Greco to make an arrest. Issue No. 4 turned the feature into a contest, offering a $25 bond to each of the first three readers to send in the correct solution. The tight dress or open blouse of the female models provides a clue as to the point of this recurring feature.

Over the Wall reports prison incidents: a shootout with guards (No. 1), prison riots (No. 2), a convict who sewed himself into a potato sack in an attempted escape on a delivery truck (No. 3), and a foiled escape from a State Reformatory caught on film (No. 4).

Crime in Cinema spotlights current movies: *The Long Wait* and *Witness to Murder* (No. 1); *Pushover* based on Thomas Walsh's *Saturday Evening Post* serial "Night Watch" (No. 2); *Black Tuesday*, a prison melodrama with Edward G. Robinson, Jean Parker, Peter Graves, and Milburn Stone (No. 3); and *Ports of Hell* with Dana Clark and Carole Matthews (No. 4).

Telecrime aka **Tele-crime** aka **Terror on TV** salutes series like *Dragnet*, *Treasury Men in Action*, *Martin Kane*, and *The Big Story* (No. 1); *Dragnet*'s Jack Webb, Ben Alexander, and "among the most promising new actresses to hit TV," Denise Vachon (No. 2); and *Danger*, *Public Defender*, and *The Lineup* (No. 4).

Issue No. 3's **Tele-Crime** provides entrée for a rant about children's programming reverting to old classics like *Peter Pan*, *Black Beauty*, and *Katzenjammer Kids* in the wake of "the recent trouble in the comic book field." [*Seduction of the Innocent* by Fredric Wertham, Rinehart, 1954.] Hence the adults are now being deprived of their evening's entertainment. "The best answer is to send the children to bed early, not to censor TV!"

Fotocrime's **Book Review** department provides only the barest of commentary on their selections, decorated by a detail from the book's cover. Their choices are: *Creep into Thy Narrow Bed* by Leonard Bishop (No. 1); *The Third Bullet* by John Dickson Carr (No. 2); *To Find a Killer* by Lionel White (No. 3); and *Cell 2455, Death Row* by Caryl Chessman (No. 4), a convicted killer who wrote his book "as an act of contrition, as a benefit to the society that shares the

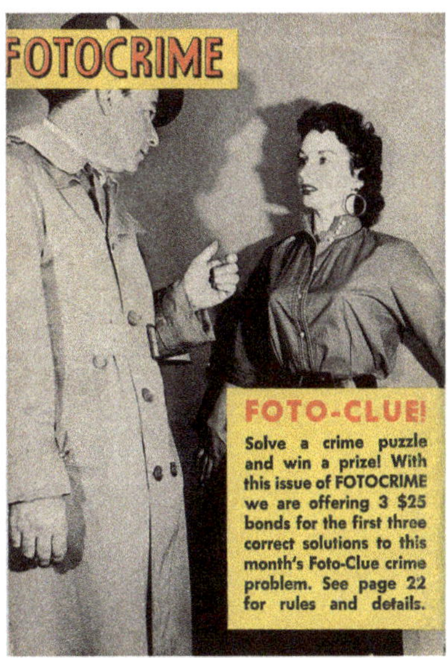

Fotocrime No. 4 May 1955, promoting the Foto-Clue contest.

responsibility for his warped soul."

Seventeen-year-old Marion Brown dropped the paperback edition of *A Kiss Before Dying* by Ira Levin (Pocket Books, 1953) during her brutal murder. *Fotocrime* grabbed onto the book's title for the name of their article on serial killer John Francis Roche. The murderer's weapons of choice were a lead pipe and a butcher knife, both found in his car after a routine traffic stop by Patrolman Gus Roniger.

Roche had six prior arrests, ranging from larceny to assault before graduating to murder, when the 28-year-old Roche began his reign of terror in New York City on November 15, 1953, robbing and stabbing 85-year-old Rosa Chronik to death in her apartment.

Four months later, he killed Marion Brown while trying to rape her. On April 16, he stabbed "Peter Jablonka, 43, in the victim's cab in

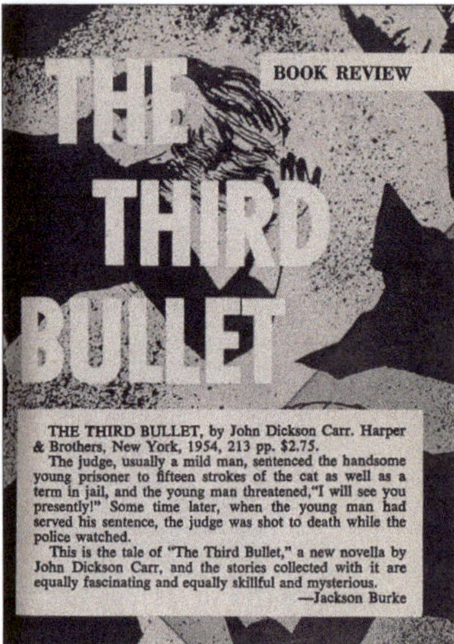

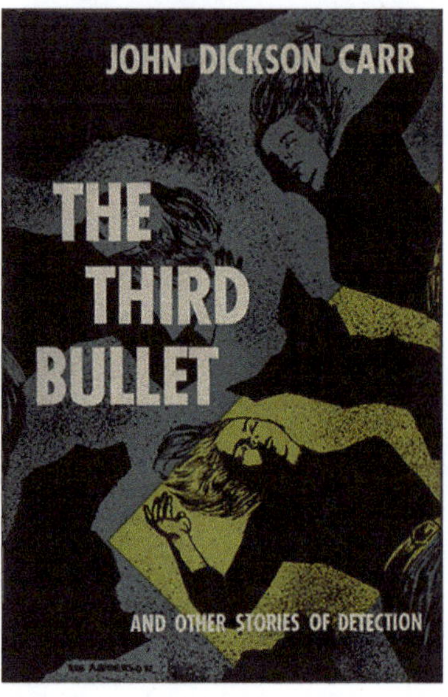

The Book Review department leveraged cover art from the books reviewed. Left: *Fotocrime* No. 2, page 57. Right: Cover art of John Dickson Carr's *The Third Bullet*.

front of the E. 22nd Street police station. Roche's body count rose to five with his final victim, 14-year-old Dorothy Westwater, whom he beat, raped, and stabbed. After his arrest, Roche confessed to all five murders. An online report notes he was electrocuted on January 26, 1956, almost a year after the last issue of *Fotocrime* appeared.

Issue No. 4 added two new departments: **Fotocrime Reconstructs a Murder!** and **Crime Classic**. The reconstruction concerns the Atkins Case, subtitled "Death and Drink." Forty-year-old Mrs. James Francis Atkins, aka Ethel May Atkins, was chopped to death in a haunted house. *Fotocrime* tracks her route on a crude map between four taverns during the three-day drunk that led to her death.

"Ethel rarely drank," her husband said, "because it affected her in an unusual way." Purportedly, after a drink or two Mrs. Atkins went off into a sort of amnesia and wound up sorry and apologetic afterward.

When questioned by police, one tavern owner identified Mrs. Atkins from a photograph and told them she'd left with Bill Earnest, George Morton, and Mary Smith. Smith's statement contradicted Earnest and Morton's, which eventually led to Earnest's confession. The men had driven Atkins to a deserted house where Earnest had "lost his head and killed Mrs. Atkins when she rebuked his advances."

A report on <casetext.com>, Commonwealth v. Earnest, Supreme Court of Pennsylvania, provides a more detailed account of the murder and replaces "George Morton" with Richard Brady. Earnest's first trial was ruled fair, the verdict just, and the penalty appropriate. He was executed in the electric chair at Rockview penitentiary, Belletontaine, PA in 1941.

Crime Classic headlines "Adulteress on Trial! The Snyder-Gray Case" in which Ruth Snyder and her lover Judd Gray bludgeoned Ruth's husband, Albert, and then strangled him with picture wire in this "tragic, morbid tale of two persons whose sexual appetites could not be satisfied."

"In her blind frenzy for love, it was never known how often and with how many men Ruth Snyder betrayed her husband. The promiscuity which she had come to need the way a vampire needs blood, led her blindly, until the moment she sat strapped and bound in the hot embrace of Sing Sing's electric chair."

Fotocrime's feature-length stories emphasized sex, serial killers, and stoking outrage. Dates were generally unreported, perhaps so readers would think older cases were breaking news.

In issue No. 1's "Red Slipper Murder Case" rookie Sheriff Dean McAllister, of Upper Sandusky, Ohio, begins an investigation after "the discovery one morning of a pathetic, crumpled body of a young woman under a stately oak tree in a deserted woods." Clad in only a nightgown and red ballet slippers, her face bludgeoned beyond recognition. The coroner's examination revealed no unique marks on her body, but she was pregnant and had recently had sexual intercourse.

When the nightgown offered McAllister no clues to the victim's identity, he scrutinized the ballet slippers and traced them to their manufacturer, discovering they had been shipped from White Plains, New York. Police there had a report of a missing 19-year-old woman,

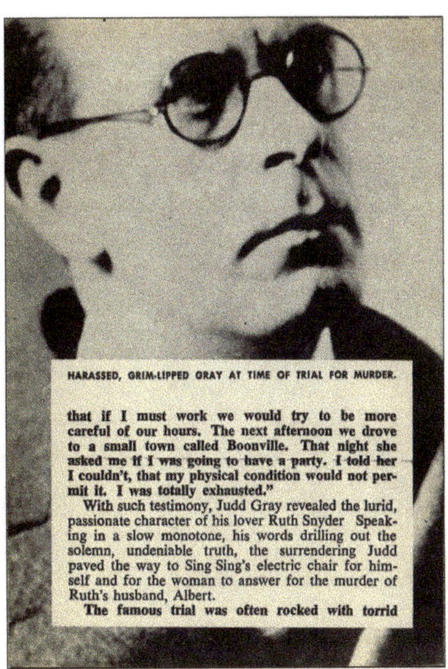

that if I must work we would try to be more careful of our hours. The next afternoon we drove to a small town called Boonville. That night she asked me if I was going to have a party. I told her I couldn't, that my physical condition would not permit it. I was totally exhausted."

With such testimony, Judd Gray revealed the lurid, passionate character of his lover Ruth Snyder Speaking in a slow monotone, his words drilling out the solemn, undeniable truth, the surrendering Judd paved the way to Sing Sing's electric chair for himself and for the woman to answer for the murder of Ruth's husband, Albert.

The famous trial was often rocked with torrid

Fotocrime No. 4, page 48 from the Crime Classic department. This page also illustrates a typcial layout--full page photo with an overlayed white box for the text.

Cynthia Pfeil, matching the general description of the victim. Pfeil's parents soon led McAllister to a boy friend, Roy Roger Schinagle, a student at Ohio Wesleyan University. McAllister picked up Schinagle and brought him to the morgue. Upon seeing Pfeil's body, Schinagle broke down and confessed to the murder.

The couple had been going steady for over a year, when Pfeil informed Schinagle she was pregnant. They planned to marry. She left home without word, following Schinagle when his new term began at Wesleyan. Unable to find a room, she spent the night in an abandoned shack where Schinagle met her. They quarreled and Schinalge, jealous of another man she knew, strangled her. Panicking, he drove her body to a deserted woods and mutilated her face so she couldn't

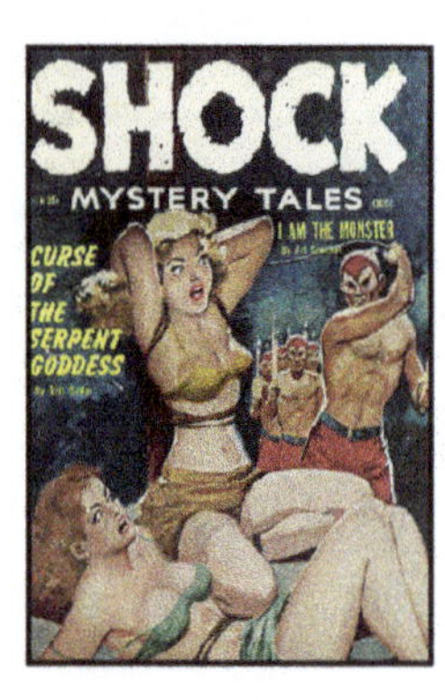

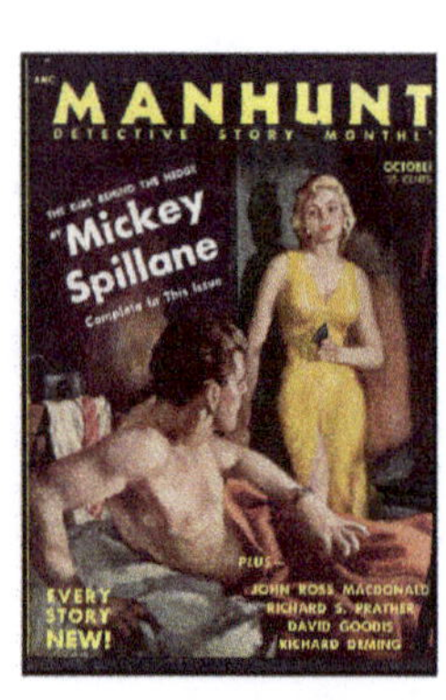

be identified. *Fotocrime* reports she was bludgeoned, but *The Daily Illini* of September 23, 1953 reports that "her face was pierced beyond recognition by more than 20 stab wounds." The paper also reports Schinagle "sobbed out a confession that covered nine typewritten pages a few hours after he was arrested on the college campus, some 40 miles south of Upper Sandusky."

Although Schinagle claimed Pfeil was the only girl in his life, McAllister found love letters from another young woman, whose identity was not revealed in the report. Schinagle, who planned to become a minister, was convicted and sentenced to life imprisonment.

Not all the crimes reported in the magazine were resolved. Issue No. 3's "Two Dead Smiths!" reports the murders of David and George Smith of the New Milford Loan Co. during a business trip with their partners, P.J. Seeley and John I. Wilke. The four men were sharing rooms at the Hotel Severs in Muskogee, Oklahoma, readying for bed, when two men suddenly entered their rooms.

When one stranger drew a gun, the brothers leapt on him but were stopped cold in a succession of four shots. Wike's who stood stunned by the proceedings, was bound and gaged, until freed by Seeley who had been in a bathroom when the attack occurred.

Muskogee police first suspected Wike and Seeley of the murder, but lack of evidence cleared them. No weapon was found. The case remained unsolved. *Fotocrime* ends their report with: "If you can tell Muskogee police who committed the murder, how the murder was committed—and make it

bring a conviction in court, you may be able to collect the more than $10,000 in reward money."

It's fair to assume *Fotocrime*'s writers had access to police reports and records, and yet many of their report's details are contradicted by information available online today.

The case of Joe Ball, an early serial killer, circa 1938, is reported in "Alligator Bait!" in issue No. 2. Ball owned the Elmendorf Tavern also known as Joe Ball's place, just off Highway 181, a dozen miles from San Antonio. Out back, he entertained "drunk-crazed" crowds feeding mongrel cats and dogs to his alligators.

When Hazel Brown, a waitress he'd hired, disappeared, her roommate, Myrna Sugg, reported her missing. Brown's mother hadn't heard from her daughter and urged police to look into the matter.

When police questioned Marvin Simpson, "a 30-year-old dimwit beer boy," who worked for Ball, he told them about a blood-stained steel barrel near the back room. When police confronted Ball, he drew a gun out of the cash drawer, "lifted the automatic against his own temple and squeezed the trigger."

Online, *Texas Monthly* provides a much more detailed account of the case, including a picture of Ball holding a whiskey bottle. *Fotocrime* ran the same photograph, but it was altered to remove the bottle.

How many women fell victim to Ball's ire is unknown, but estimates range from five to as high as 25. As *Texas Monthly* surmises: ". . . the hype kept building and the mistakes repeating: how Ball shot himself in the head, how his handyman was named Wilfred Sneed, how Sneed

Left: Photo of Joe Ball from *Fotocrime* No. 2 and Right: the same photo from *Texas Monthly* online, showing the whiskey bottle.

said that he had cut up twenty women, how chunks of human flesh were found in the pool. In retrospect, it's hard to tell whom to trust." Those who want more facts than *Texas Monthly* provides online, may want to track down *The Wild and Free Dukedom of Bexar* by Elton Cude, Jr. son of the Bexar County deputy sheriff who helped with the original investigation.

Another serial killer struck in issue No. 2's "The 'Good' Killer," that leads with the brutal murder of Mary Babcock. Her killer struck again and again at girls and women from ages 12 to 22. But his attacks were not all successful. Betty Swenson was saved when her cries for help drove her attacker to escape through a window. When 14-year-old Mary Donnell came to Mercy Hospital bruised, with a broken ice pick stuck in her back, police finally had an eye wit-

ness. The arrest and conviction of "model boy" Tom Smith followed quickly. As did his life sentence.

As a young man, Ben Hecht became a noted journalist before moving on to even greater success as an author, playwright, screen writer, director and producer. In issue's No. 3's "Ben Hecht Cracks Crime" Carl Wanderer and his wife Ruth walk home from a movie one evening in June. Neighbors, sitting on their verandas, later recalled seeing a strange figure following the couple to their apartment. As the pair entered their building "a man in tattered clothes suddenly jumped from behind and began shooting wildly."

The stranger fired at Ruth, snatching her purse, and then turned on Carl. But Carl carried his own gun, a Colt .45, which he drew and shot the stranger until the man fell heavily to the floor. When neighbor James Williams came to see what was happening he found Carl, "insane with hate and fear bent over the dead man, knocking the man's head repeatedly against the floor."

Carl Wanderer's account of the assault seemed believable to Sgt. Michael Grady, and the local newspapers echoed outrage at the tragic deaths of Ruth and the couple's unborn child. The Chicago press dubbed the killer "The Ragged Stranger."

However, when reporter Ben Hecht approached Wanderer for an interview, the widower's demeanor changed the moment he realized he had an audience. When Hecht told Sgt. Grady about the odd encounter, it was enough for the Sgt. to launch a full-fledged investigation.

Turns out, Wanderer had not been happy to learn his wife was

Fotocrime No. 2 February 1955.

pregnant. "He was involved in a love affair with a buxom brunette." He told Ruth to withdraw all their money from the bank. "Then he scoured skid-row until he found a tattered, starving bum who agreed to follow the Wanderers home, draw a gun and scare them, 'just as a joke.'"

As the prank unfolded, Wan-derer shot his wife in the heart and the abdomen, before unloading the Colt on his tragic dupe. When confronted with this version of events, Wanderer admitted the plot and was arrested.

The report on <CrimeMagazine.com> by Benjamin Welton differs on nearly every detail of the case, although the major facts align. Welton reports Wanderer was tried twice and finally sentenced to death by hanging, which was carried out on September 30, 1921.

Feel like today's society is out of control? So did 1950s readers of *Fotocrime*—and the magazine was happy to add fuel to the fire. In "City Gone Mad" (No. 1) a "Crime Wave in Dallas" breaks 26 years of "the most peaceful community in the Lone Star State." There are no pat answers or resolutions in *Fotocrime*'s exposé. A rampage of rape and 43 murders have so alarmed the locals that "Armed citizens got out their shooting irons and peppered the night air with buckshot and bullets at the slightest suspicion of prowlers."

A few pages later, we learn murder is the consequence of mail order guns in "These Guns for Sale!" New York State's 1911 gun control legislation, the Sullivan Act, is rendered ineffective by every one of over a dozen mail order houses specializing in instruments of death. "Only $19.50—Double Action revolver, worth more, .32 or .38 cal. Nickel or blue finish. Powerful and hardhitting," reads a typical 2-inch advertisement. *Fotocrime* attributes nearly half-a-dozen murders to mail order guns—from gangland mobsters to domestic tragedies.

In issue No. 2, "Stir Crazy!" ignites concerns about a massive prison break unleashing thousands of prisoners "maddened by confinement, sex-starved, anxious for vengeance . . . It wouldn't be pretty."

Such a large-scale event nearly happened in Jackson, Michigan when inmates rioted and "came within a half-hour" of breaking out en masse. *Fotocrime* reports the top four reasons prisoners are stir crazy: Poor chow, overcrowding, favoritism, and poor administration.

"As an insider I can warn you that unless these penal problems are cleaned up, there will be a jailbreak one day that may make a bloody shambles of an entire country before it is quelled."

Decades before Ted Kaczynski, a disgruntled miner named Michael Fugmann constructed and mailed six cigar box bombs to citizens of Wilkes-Barre, Pennsylvania. According to issue No. 3's "The Good Friday Bombing!" he took his motive to the electric chair. The report claims "His choice of victims followed no clear pattern and no one was safe from the terror that came in the mail!"

If truly random, how did Fugmann become suspect number one? Bomb experts examined all the evidence from the bombs, including three that had been intercepted after "Wilkes-Barre police impounded all mail at the post office!" Next, they "seized nails from the houses of all the victims' friends and acquaintances. Their search found matching nails in the home of a friend of victim Thomas Maloney's."

According to a more lucid report at <citizensvoice.com>, "Fugmann had reason to be angry with all" of his victims and intended victims. All were involved with the coal mining industry and Fugmann felt the mines had thwarted his union's attempts to improve working conditions and benefits. Once all the players' roles were known, it wouldn't have taken the police long to identify Fugmann as a key suspect. Fugmann claimed innocence through the end, but the circumstantial evidence of his handwriting, wood, nails, glue, and wrapping paper all supported his guilt. He was executed on July 17, 1938.

Fotocrime No. 4 includes two cautionary tales. "All sorts of fancy highbrow psychological theories have been advanced to 'explain' why young kids from fairly decent homes would turn killers, prowl dark Brooklyn streets and viciously swoop down on unsuspecting and helpless elderly victims." These are "New York's Thrill Killers!" Led by Jack Koslow, their "skinny pinch-faced" gang leader, Brooklyn's "Thrill Kids" tortured and murdered their hapless victim. *Fotocrime*'s report compares them to gangsters like "Legs" Diamond, Killer Cole, Baby-Face Nelson, and Machine-Gun Kelly, none who would ever dare launch an attack unless their gangs vastly outnumbered their victims.

Later in that same issue, *Fotocrime* cites three cases of children killing one or both of their parents as the supporting evidence to their chilling cautionary tale, "Will Your Kid Kill You?"

"Are these children who slew their own mothers and fathers exceptions, or will your child, too, turn on his parents with cyanide, an axe, or a rifle? Is street-corner society breaking down family ties so that your son will forget to love you? And then kill you?"

Beginning with issue No. 2, the contents page declares *Fotocrime* & *Suspect* "Two Magazines in One!" A search of the catalog site True Crime Detective Magazines reveals no prior *Suspect* magazine to join *Fotocrime*. Issue No. 4 raises the ante with an announcement at the bottom of the contents page: "To all readers of FOTOCRIME: In the near future SUSPECT magazine will appear as a large-size magazine! Look for SUSPECT at your favorite newsstand!"

Still, I can find no record of a *Suspect* true crime magazine. In November 1955 a crime fiction digest appeared called *Suspect Detective Stories*, from a different publisher, NY address, and staff than *Fotocrime*. *Suspect Detective Stories* lasted five issues, ending in October 1956.

Fotocrime hired models for their covers and crime reenactment features, but none are identified. Issue No. 3's Tele-Crime segment includes a photo of "TV talent" June Randy. She looks to me like the model on the cover of issue No. 2 and the woman in a reenactment photo for "The Beast of the Autobahn" in issue No. 3. The website <pulpinternational.com> reports images of American burlesque dancers, including June Randy, in the Sept. 1954 issue of pocket-size magazine *Dare*. Perhaps her acting gigs were aspirational; a search on IMDb scored no results.

Some of the coverage suggests Burke and Machlin used whatever they had on hand. Issue No. 1's "Murder Wears Short Pants" presents a disjointed two-page spread. The captions of its two photos read: "Bobby Munday explains 'accidental' hanging of three-year old Tommy Laux." and "Dick Pruitt, 16, confessed killer." Yet, the report below it centers on fifteen-year-old Louis Maus, Jr. who was found hanged in the cellar of Giuseppe Raio's grocery in Brooklyn. Reported as a suicide, yet the rope pinion-

Fotocrime No. 3 March 1955.

ing his arms seems to refute that theory. Why the photographs and story don't match up is baffling.

Also in issue No. 1 is a story called "He Killed to Eat." Inside, the cover blurb, "Ballerina and the Bluebeard" became its subtitle. An American dancer, Jean De Koven, was strangled by Eugene "Siegfried" Weidmann, who claimed he killed her and his other five victims for the money he removed from their purses and wallets. *Fotocrime* reports his motive, "Money to Eat," which became their headline. In total Weidmann killed six times for just $625. According to *Fotocrime* his take from De Koven was only "the small change she had in her handbag."

However, Wikipedia's entry

Suspect Detective Stories Vol. 1 No. 1 November 1955. Cover by Robert Engle.

on Weidmann states he took 300 francs in cash and $430 in traveller's cheques. He also sent a ransom demand for $500 to De Koven's aunt for her return.

Two years later, Weidman's execution by guillotine in June 1939 was notable as the last public execution in France, although the practice continued in private until 1977. According to <mashable.com>, in attendance for Weidman's beheading was future star Christopher Lee, then 17 years old.

One of issue No. 2's cover stories, "Love Killers!" was subtitled "Sex Behind the Barn! The Hired Hand Hired a Gun." Purportedly, only Carl Baglien knew his wife Martha "was having sex forays with handsome 21-year-old Egil Kjella," his hired hand. When concerned neighbors called police about Baglien's sudden disappearance from his farm, investigators soon pieced together the facts. Martha had given Kjella's slow-witted brother Martin, $40 to buy a gun which he used to kill Baglien and buried his body in a shallow grave on the property. "Mrs. Baglien didn't deny her part. 'It was wrong and I have suffered. I think I'm pregnant, and if I am Egil is the father.'" All three went sent to jail for murder.

Subsequent research often contradicts *Fotocrime*'s reports, but sometimes the magazine even contradicted itself. "The Beast of the Autobahn" is illustrated primarily with reenactment photos in issue No. 3. The report's opening lines state the victim was "beaten, stripped, and raped" yet their following account contradicts two of their own assertions.

A beautiful 22-year-old redhead meets a middle-aged gentleman in a Frankfurt cafe and agrees to have dinner with him. They drive through the city chatting amiably until they reach the outskirts of town, where "he steps on the gas and sped down the Autobahn as if demons pursued him."

He refuses to answer his passenger's repeated questions, remaining silent until he pulls off the highway alongside a clump of trees and lunges for her. As she tries to escape, he whips out a pistol and orders her disrobe. As she strips, he becomes more and more excited, his hand shaking violently as she removes her final article of clothing. At this moment, she leaps from the Mercedes and bolts down the road. The Beast fires wildly and misses her several times until she is out of range. Rather than leave his car unattended while chasing her on foot, he escapes the scene in a spray of gravel.

The naked redheaded beauty is rescued by a truck driver who delivers her to a police station, where she gives her statement. (The report leaves readers to assume she's given something to cover herself at some point during her rescue.)

The Autobahn Beast had struck less than six weeks earlier, strangling pretty 18-year-old Christa Eggert and leaving her body by the side of the superhighway near Hanover.

Fotocrime reports no resolution to the manhunt for this rapist-slayer, but offers the experts their own analysis.

1: Strangling indicates incredible strength.

2: Each rape includes murder and therefore must be the work of the same man.

3: Witnesses testify to several models of sports cars, therefore the murder is a man of means.

4: All the crimes occurred along the Autobahn, so it's likely the suspect is a traveling man, most likely a salesman.

Conclusion: "A thorough check-up on all traveling salesmen along the autobahn route can be done through those businesses that have salesmen along this route, and the result will inevitably lead to the Beast of the Autobahn."

In the same issue, "Mother was a Tattoo!" opens with a deadly account: "The nude body of blonde, seductive Shirley Scott was jammed tightly into the small hotel closet." Soon, it's revealed. "On the thighs of both her gorgeous legs, Shirley had tattoos! The left one was of a woman with long hair, and banner etched around the form read: 'MOTHER.' On the right leg was a red and blue tattoo of the Statue of Liberty."

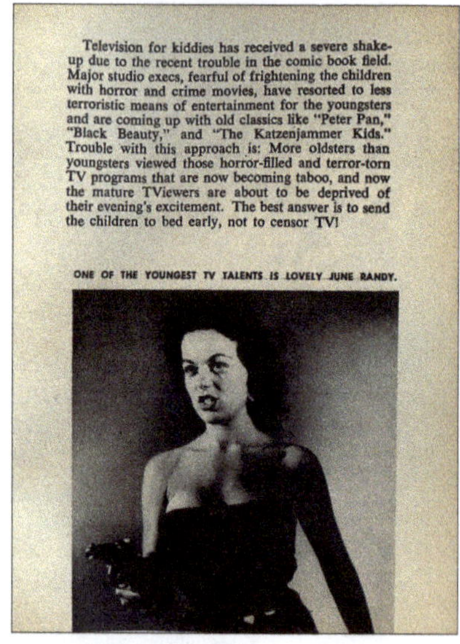

Fotocrime No. 3's Tele-Crime department with alledged TV actress June Randy.

Ray Clawson, Senior Detective of Ogden, Utah learned from a desk clerk the murderer had been dressed as a sailor and was smoking a black cigar when the couple registered at the hotel. Clawson's first suspect was Scott's husband, but learned from the U.S. Navy he'd been at sea for the past month. As the investigation progressed, Clawson uncovered an attack by a cigar-smoking sailor in Pocatello, Idaho, and the rape of a telephone operator in Butte, Montana who described a similar perpetrator.

Remarkably, an Ogden cab driver who'd read of the murder in the local newspaper called police when his fare matched the description. Richard Pax was soon arrested and confessed to the Scott murder under pressure, "I got mad when she asked me for fifty dollars. I knocked her down. Women get me crazy when they get on my nerves."

No mention is made of the

Fotocrime No. 4 May 1955.

Pax's conviction or sentence, but the similar crimes in Pocatello and Butte turned out to be unrelated.

The final crime in our report comes from issue No. 2: "Death was a Left-Hander!" and "The 'A-Bomb' Killer!" Helen Beavers, a 26-year-old waitress from the Good Luck cafe in Duncan, Oklahoma, was discovered by W.C. Gentry in the trunk of his car shortly after he returned home from his hospital stay in Oklahoma City, 80-some miles away.

Police doggedly followed every lead and questioned three suspects, going as far as arresting one who was identified by Beavers' girl friend, Joyce King, who claimed she saw him bludgeoning Beavers, but later repudiated her statement.

An arrest was finally made when a report from Wichita Falls came in. "Lefty" Fowler had been arrested on a drunk charge and spoke about a murder in Duncan, although at that time no body had been found.

Duncan police knew of an E.L. Fowler who had resigned from the police force several days before Beavers' body was found. When medical x-ray evidence indicated the killer had been left-handed, Fowler confessed. Frustrated at Beavers' refusal to accommodate him, Fowler struck her with an "atom bomb," aka a "slapper," a small metal disk inserted in the lining of his glove and held in the palm of his hand.

In the bloody reenactment photo of Beavers' body in the trunk of a car she is wearing underwear, whereas *Fotocrime*'s report states she was "minus her bra and panties." Fowler's guilt for the crime was unequivocal.

However, further research shows the crime occurred in 1948. A few years later famed mystery writer and trial lawyer, Erle Stanley Gardner, partnered with Henry Steeger, publisher of *Argosy*, to analyze the trial's transcripts for their series: The Court of Last Resort. The Beavers' case was riddled with doubts, and Fowler's confessions were clearly coerced. Harry Henderson along with photographer Walt Wiggins, and the Last Court's chief investigator Tom Smith, reported their exhaustive investigation in the pages of *Argosy* in January 1952. No "slapper" is mentioned. The murder weapon may have been a twelve-inch wrench. Henderson's eight-page report would have been available to *Fotocrime*'s writer, had he looked.

Erle Stanley Gardner wrote further about Fowler in his compilation named for the series, *The Court of Last Resort* in 1952 (revised in 1954). In Gardner's report he presents numerous bits of evidence that point to Fowler's wrongful conviction. ". . . things that are disclosed by Fowler's petition before the Board of Pardon and Parole, and it will be interesting to see what happens."

Well, the wheels of justice... According to <victimsofthestate.org> "In 1960, Fowler was granted habeas corpus relief due to his coerced and illegal interrogation. He presumably was released."

Fotocrime is a good example of the whole being greater than the sum of its parts. Despite its sloppy reporting it provides a solid resource for identifying over a dozen shocking murders and some early serial killers. Although its sensationalist approach stoked reader's fears of thrill killers and terrorists, it does provide a record of those mid-1950s fears. Its prison coverage was insignificant except for recording prisoners' top four complaints, which provide a chilling reminder of how little has changed. Today, *Fotocrime*'s pocket-size format, gaudy covers, bare-bones design, and tawdry stories make it a fascinating, kitschy, true crime collectible. Secondary booksellers may ask upwards of $50 a copy, but patience can yield results for $10–$15 an issue.

Stark House Press

LORENZ HELLER WRITING
AS FREDERICK LORENZ

A Rage at Sea /
A Party Every Night
978-1-944520-99-1 $19.95

Sabotage at sea leads to dangerous
adventure, and a bartender with a past
becomes an unwitting murder suspect—
two classic 1950's crime stories
originally published by Lion Books.
New introduction by Nicholas Litchfield.
May 2020.

DOUGLAS SANDERSON WRITING
AS MALCOLM DOUGLAS

Prey by Night /
Rain of Terror
978-1-951473-00-6 $19.95

Two fast and furious Gold Medal classics.
"One of the most exciting and delightfully
romantic adventure yarns we've ever
read."—*The Naperville Sun*. Introduction
by Gregory Shepard. June 2020.

STARK HOUSE PRESS
1315 H Street, Eureka, CA 95501
707-498-3135 www.StarkHousePress.com
Available from your local bookstore, or direct from the publisher.

PulpFest 2021

Report by Mike Chomko and William Lampkin

For the first time, *The Pulpster*, the annual publication for the summer's convention for fans of vintage popular fiction and related collectibles, will come out without a convention.

Since September 2019, the PulpFest organizing committee had been hard at work, planning and promoting their 49th summertime pulp convention. Guests and presenters had been lined up, advertisements designed and printed, and numerous posts had been assigned and written. The winter holidays arrived and everything seemed fine . . . except in China. Countless people were becoming seriously ill from a new virus. Many were dying.

On March 12, 2020, the World Health Organization declared a global outbreak of the COVID-19 virus. By the middle of May, there were over five million confirmed cases worldwide and nearly 340,000 deaths. Everyday living across the entire planet came to a halt as people were urged to "shelter in place."

For the last several years, PulpFest was staged at the Double-Tree by Hilton Hotel Pittsburgh—Cranberry in Mars, Pennsylvania. Although it is likely that businesses and events in the region would be allowed to resume operations in June, they would have been required to follow guidelines issued by the United States Centers for Disease Control and Prevention and the Pennsylvania Department of Health.

Included in the CDC's guidelines are recommendations that large gatherings should be canceled. Given the substantial risks involved and the desire to maintain the health and safety of the convention's many supporters, the PulpFest organizing committee voted unanimously to postpone this year's gathering until early August 2021.

Typically, all PulpFest members receive a complimentary copy of the convention's program book, *The Pulpster*. But this year because of the con's cancellation, the magazine's 29th annual edition will be available for purchase later in the summer.

The Pulpster grew out of a conversation at Pulpcon 19 (the predecessor of PulpFest) in 1990.

Tony Davis, the magazine's founding editor, recalls:

Preliminary cover of *The Pulpster* No. 29 with artwork by Margaret Brundage.

"Don Hutchison and I drove from Toronto, and on arrival and registration I was handed a folded sheet of colored paper with the convention agenda and some guest of honor information. That's it? That's the convention guide?

"I later asked (Pulpcon organizer) Rusty Hevelin about it, and he told me about time, effort, and expenses, and then I said to him (O foolish me) that I'd be prepared to edit a convention zine. We'll see, he replied.

"For a few weeks after Pulpcon I solicited material from individuals I'd met at the convention such as Bob Sampson, Al Tonik, Will Murray, Nick Carr, and John Wooley, and contacted Rusty with my plan. Some money was set aside for a program book, and the rest is history."

The Pulpster debuted as a 44-page octavo-size magazine,

The Pulpster No. 3 July/Aug. 1993.
Cover by Paul McCall.

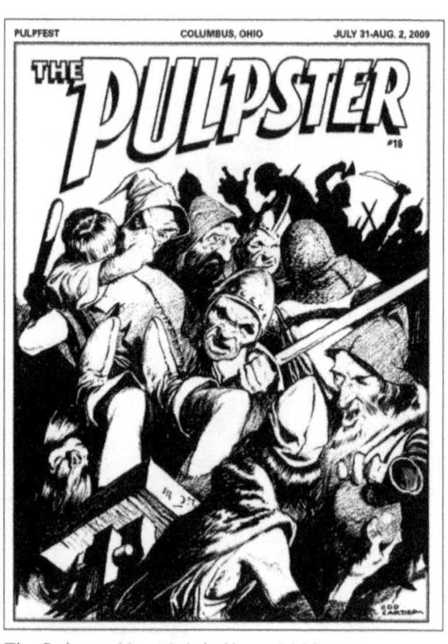

The Pulpster No. 18 July/Aug. 2009.
Cover by Edd Cartier.

commonly called a chapbook, at Pulpcon 20. The first issue featured a wrap-around cover by Franklyn E. Hamilton, and articles by all of those mentioned by Davis.

It returned the next year, again as the octavo size (5.5-inches by 8.5-inches), but grew to quarto size (or letter size, 8.5-inches by 11-inches) with issue number 3 in 1993. It's remained that size since.

With number 18 in 2009, *The Pulpster* saw a major change. With the demise of Pulpcon, the magazine moved to its successor, PulpFest.

In 2010, *The Pulpster* appeared with its first full-color cover, a reproduction of the cover of September 1929 number of *Black Mask* magazine by H.C. Murphy and promoting the appearance of Dashiell Hammett's "The Maltese Falcon."

Tony Davis remained editor through issue number 21 in 2012, marking 22 years. He continues contributing to *The Pulpster* with the Final Chapters department, providing tributes to pulpsters and fans who have passed away in recent times; and with articles.

Beginning with number 22, William Lampkin, proprietor of <ThePulp.Net> and who has been designing *The Pulpster* since number 17, became its editor.

The Pulpster now typically runs 52 pages, with color covers. It continues to boast articles by some of the biggest names in pulp history and research, including Murray, Hutchinson, Ron Goulart, Bill Pronzini, John Locke, Jeffrey Shanks, Don Herron, Garyn Roberts, Mike Chomko, Laurie Powers, Nathan Vernon Madison, Monte Herridge, and more, and has featured original illustrations by Hamilton, Francesco Francavilla, and Kez Wilson.

The 2020 issue will explore a variety of topics that would have been themes at this year's PulpFest. This year marks the 100th an-

The Pulpster No. 19 July/Aug. 2010.
Cover by H.C. Murphy.

The Pulpster No. 22 July 2013.
Cover by Walter M. Baumhofer.

niversary of the birth of author Ray Bradbury. Professor Garyn Roberts will offer several articles on Bradbury, with emphasis on his pulp magazine contributions.

Pulp historian and writer Will Murray examines *Black Mask* on the magazine's 100th anniversary. The Pulpster will also feature an excerpt from *Joseph T. Shaw: The Man Behind Black Mask*, the biography of the magazine's most influential editor, "Cap" Shaw, written by his son, Milton Shaw. And Bob Deis and Wyatt Doyle, editors of Men's Adventure Library Journal and authors of the book *Eva: Men's Adventure Supermodel*, profile model, pin-up, and actress Eva Lynd.

But *The Pulpster* also looks beyond the PulpFest themes this year, with several additional articles. Editor emeritus Tony Davis writes about Thomas P. Kelley, the self-declared "King of the Canadian Pulp Writers." Pulp historian Darrell

Schweitzer provides an interview he conducted with SF authors and husband-and-wife Edmond Hamilton and Leigh Brackett.

Author Stuart Hopen recalls a meeting with author Philip Wylie, whose novels inspired a number of pulp and popular culture characters, including Doc Savage, Flash Gordon, and Superman. Martin Grams celebrates the 100th anniversary of Renfrew of the Royal Mounted, a popular boy's adventure series that expanded into magazines, radio, film, and television.

Rounding out the issue is the department, Final Chapters.

Watch for details regarding purchasing *The Pulpster* at the magazine's website <thepulpster.com>, or on the PulpFest website <pulpfest.com>.

bare•bones No. 1
Review by Richard Krauss

After years of reboots, the brain trust of Peter Enfantino and John Scoleri has risen again from the black fountain and is now back in print with a brand new take on "unearthing vintage, forgotten and overlooked horror/mystery/sci-fi/western/weird film, paperbacks, comics, pulp fiction, and video." You can read more backstory in Peter and John's "Dueling Editorials" that kick off the issue.

Mucking About in the Mouse Auditorium by Thomas Deja
An Introduction to that "Swinging Private Dick," Ed Noon—The Worst Detective Ever Created.

To use the analogy Deja himself conjures up for his article—think Ed Wood. Pop culture so bad, you can't stop watching—or in this case—reading. At least that's what I walked away with from Deja's loving, but brutally honest appraisal of the Ed Noon series of an astonishing 31 paperback novels, churned out by the prolific Michael Avallon starting in 1953 and ending 1998, the year Avallon died.

Deja intersperses backstory with synopses of several of Noon's adventures in this fascinating article that's just the right length and tone. I loved learning all I ever wanted to know about this "Swinging Private Dick" and grateful for the tip-off to never actually read one. Co-editor Peter Enfantino provides a complete list of Noon's novels (published and unpublished) for your masochistic pleasure.

Red Planet Hollywood
by Matthew R. Bradley
The Martian Chronicles on Screen.

Adapted from Bradley's *Richard Matheson on Screen: A History of the Filmed Works*, an exhaustively researched recap of Ray Bradbury's *The Martian Chronicles* reimagined for big and small screens. The most successful adaptation for a TV series is given particular attention—all supported with

bare•bones

Number 1   Winter 2020

quotes from Bradley's interviews with Ray Bradbury himself.

A Fistful of Fury
by Thomas W. Flynn, Jr.
The Spaghetti Western/Martial Arts Mash-Ups of the 1970s.

No question Flynn knows his flicks. His overview of the "genre" and synopses of select pics and pans are jam-packed with context and supporting referentials. This is the kind of exploration I find fascinating to read about and yet have no desire to wade through the movies themselves. Kudos to Flynn for screening out all the boring parts in his well-illustrated 18-page report.

Born of I Am Legend by John Scoleri

Tracing the lineage of Richard Matheson's *I Am Legend* to George Romero's *Night of the Living Dead*.

For some, the connection between Matheson's hit novel and Romero's hit movie is old news, but Scoleri's article, expanded from its earlier appearance in *50 Years of Night: Night of the Living Dead—The Official Magazine* (Fantasm Media, 2018), provides ample detail of the connection, including quotes from those with first hand knowledge. As Scoleri surmises, "Matheson's novel focuses on themes of loneliness, isolation, and ultimately self-realization, whereas *Night of the Living Dead* deals with the breakdown of society, and how a small group fails to come together in a time of crisis."

Swords, Sorcery, Savagery, and Civilization by Gilbert Colon

Book Two of Lin Carter's "People of the Dragon" Saga.

First published in the Dec. 1977 issue of *Fantastic*, "The People of the Dragon" launched the start of a promising "dragon" series, supported by an illustration by Tony Gleeson. "It is forgotten because only two stories in, [the second was "The Pillars of Hell"] Carter abandoned it (as he did many projects)." Colon provides character sketches and the basic story arc, along with its subsequent printings, for this forgotten but worthwhile series.

Digging into Crime Digests

by Peter Enfantino

Alfred Hitchcock's Mystery Magazine and *Justice*.

Not a fan of the private eye genre, ala Mike Shayne and Shell Scott, Enfantino finds plenty to like outside PI tropes in the early *Hitchcock's* and the short lived *Justice* crime digests. After an overview of each title, he selects a favorite issue of each run and delves into its best stories.

Christian Stavrakis: The *bare•bones* Interview

by John Scoleri

Stavrakis is a sculptor, filmmaker, and rabid fan of everything George A. Romero. His bronze bust of Romero is displayed in the Monroeville Mall where *Dawn of the Dead* was filmed. He's part of the audio commentary track on a DVD version of the film, webmaster of the original LivingDead.com, and an author. Scoleri's initial 2001 interview was augmented in 2019 to include Stavrakis' most recent projects. It's a fascinating conversation; Stavrakis' work is worth bragging about, yet he strikes me as humble, enthusiastic, and generous.

Doorways to Darkness

by J. Charles Burwell

A Survey of Key Hardboiled/Noir Anthologies.

Like many fans of hardboiled fiction, Burwell's journey began with Hammett and Chandler, which led to *Black Mask*, Joseph T. Shaw's *The Hardboiled Omnibus* and Geoffrey O'Brien's *Hardboiled America*. The latter being a history of the field and many of its most notable authors. Having set the stage, Burwell reviews several top-tier anthologies, beginning with Shaw's *Omnibus*. The reviews provide an excellent representation of what readers can expect, and of course, all of them are essential for students of the genre.

Here's the list: Will Oursler's *As Tough As They Come* (Perma, 1951), Ron Goulart's *The Hardboiled Dicks* (Sherbourne Press, 1965; Pocket Books, 1967), William F. Nolan's *The Black Mask Boys: Masters of the Hard-Boiled School of Detective Fiction* (William Morris and Co.,1985; Mysterious Press, 1987), Bill Pronzini and Jack Adrian's *Hard-Boiled: An Anthology of American Crime Stories* (Oxford University Press, 1995); and Edward Gorman's *The Black Lizard Anthology of Crime Fiction* (Black Lizard Books, 1987). And so as to not leave anyone behind, Burwell closes with a supplemental list of five more heavy hitters.

Sleaze Alley by Peter Enfantino

Racy covers and steamy sex from a stream of second-tier publishers gave birth to the sleaze wave of paperback originals. Many beginning writers honed their craft in the sleaze milieu and went on to fame in more respectable genres like crime and science fiction. In this issue, Enfantino gives us an up-close, candid view into five sleaze PBOs from the 1960s: *Lust Crew* by Robert Silverberg writing as Don Elliott, *The Lustful Ones* by William Knoles writing as Clyde Allison, *Sin Gun* by J.X. Williams, *Sin Quest* by Robert Silverberg writing as Don Elliott, and *Lover, Destroy Me* by William F. Frank. With detailed plot synopsis, cover art, and juicy extracts from each selection, Enfantino provides everything you need to know about just how far—and how far gone— these paperbound beauties will go.

What's on the Tube? by John Scoleri
TV Guide Flashback: January 1–7, 1972 (San Francisco Edition).

In the entertainment biz, con-cept is king. Scoleri hits pay dirt, grabbing a back issue of yesterday's essential television companion, *TV Guide*, and scouring its pages for gold. He shares his thoughts as well as the original program descriptions of the best the week has to offer from the big networks and the local station's pre- and post-prime time broadcasts. Great fun.

R&D: Walk My Plank by David J. Schow

Ever wonder about the writing credits way up there on the silver screen? Schow takes us behind the scenes and explains how we got where we are and advocates for an expanded "Participating Writers" credit, reflecting today's productions which typically involve a half-dozen or more.

About the Contributors

You might be tempted to skip the contributor bios—don't. This batch is a bit more detailed than many I've seen and it's quite helpful to understand where *b*•*b*'s writers come from. The final few pages consist of ads—some vintage and some hawking other Cimarron Street Books.

Like its contributors, the return of *bare*•bones offers an eclectic mix with impressive range. Even when one of its many topics is not of primary interest to you, its presentation and depth of coverage provide an enjoyable, edifying lesson in pop culture.

Separation

Fiction by Joe Wehrle, Jr.
Collage by Marc Myers

The small black duffel bag hit the beach house floor as if it symbolized an accomplished fact. He'd never used the bag except when he was on his own, as he certainly was now.

The lights worked and the toilet flushed, that was good. The small stove would heat up, too, he supposed, but he would probably be eating out. There was a little

diner just off the tourist track that a lot of the locals patronized.

A memory of morning scrambled eggs with spinach and cheese and something tomatoey (the special way she made them) flashed through his mind, complete with taste and smell, but he dismissed it abruptly and began sorting through the dresser drawers to see what they'd left there last time. He put the black duffel on top of the dresser because he didn't feel like unpacking it just then.

The brochures from their vacation were carefully stacked in the bottom drawer. He wondered why she had kept them. Probably because they'd both forgotten the camera, and there were pictures of the hotel and of other attractions at the resort.

Well, *there* was something he hadn't seen before, or hadn't remembered. With a black marker she had cartooned figures of them on the restaurant photo, celebrating the hilarious confrontation they'd had with the waiter. She hadn't had to draw the waiter in, as the brochure actually showed him standing by a table, suggesting a ready-to-serve attitude, but she had drawn them seated in such a way as to make it look like he was giving them the cold shoulder. The image precipitated a laugh which he cut short as he replaced the pile in the drawer.

He looked around for something to read, and found the old collection of Wodehouse stories. She always laughed when he read her passages from them in a fake British accent. Not what he wanted today, though. Underneath the Wodehouse was a John D. MacDonald, *Dead Low Tide*, he'd never got around to reading. That was more like it.

He laid the book on the table beside the comfortable chair she'd recovered in corduroy (the original cloth had felt too scratchy when you were wearing beach shorts), and he went to see what was in the small refrigerator.

There was a six-pack of ale and one loose bottle of Guinness. That's right, the Ennis couple they met at the Cleveland convention brought Guinness when they visited that weekend in April. He had most of it over the next few days, but saved the last one for her. They always said they'd keep Guinness in the refrigerator all the time when they hit it big. Which hadn't happened yet. They only had the beach house because his grandfather Ben had left it to them, and they had talked about selling it to reduce their debt, but there were . . . memories that still kept them from doing it. He reached for the Guinness, then set it back and pulled out one of the ales.

The bottle was two-thirds empty and he'd read fourteen pages of his book when he set it down and drummed his fingers on the table for a couple of minutes, looking out the window across from where he was sitting.

He remembered he hadn't checked for a dial tone on the phone. He picked it up and put it to his ear. There was a tone all right.

It hadn't quite touched the cradle when he suddenly brought it back and started punching in the numbers for his house. She answered on the second ring, and he thought her voice sounded lonely. "Hello?"

John Shirley on Weirdbook No. 42

Interviewed by Richard Krauss

This review/interview combines a synopsis of each story followed by John Shirley's comments, conducted in mid-March 2020.

The long-waited issue No. 42 of *Weirdbook* is a special edition filled entirely with the stories and works of John Shirley. Editor Doug Draa sets the tone in his introduction, "I first read Mr. Shirley's 'City Come A Walkin' right after going into the Army back in 1980. I've been a huge fan ever since."

The Digest Enthusiast: What was the catalyst for this special issue and how did it take shape?

John Shirley: I had a sword-and-sorcery novella about heroic and sorcerous doings in Atlantis, a tale I didn't really have a market for. It was too short to be sold as a novel and too long for most markets and few of them take fantasy. So I thought of *Weirdbook*, which specializes in fiction a la "*Weird Tales* Magazine," from way back in the day, and they were delighted to have the piece. The editor Douglas Draa is a bit of a fan of mine. So he suggested that since it was such a long piece they could do a special John Shirley edition if I had other pieces to reprint. I had a couple of stories I had to yet try placing and some lesser known pieces that were relevant to the publication and they took those and a selection of some of my weird poetry. I've taken to writing rhyming poetry reminiscent of Lovecraft's "Fungi from Yuggoth" (as one example), but with my own themes— also a couple of those poems are also song lyrics. Since I'm a songwriter too, writing lyrics for the Blue Oyster Cult and Blue Coupe and my own bands, and much of it being of *Weird Tales* flavored, it fit . . .

TDE: The book opens with "Anvil Rock," a story in which a Gold Mine magnate named Grigsby begins to regret the criminal and murderous things he's done to make his fortune. But what really torments his soul is the agony of premonition—knowing what's coming and feeling powerless to stop it. How did Grisby and

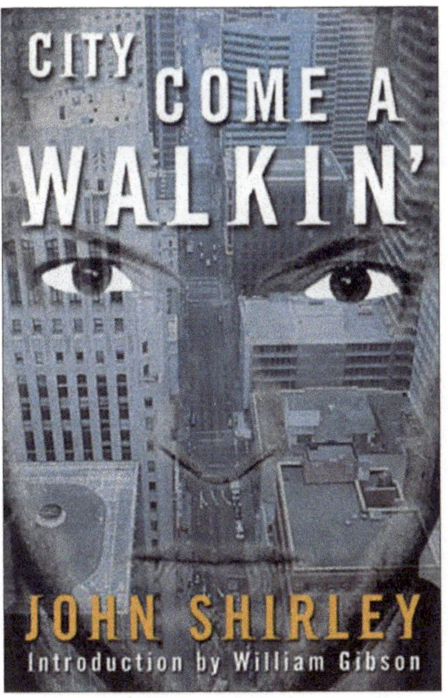

his personal purgatory develop?

JS: We all have regrets. I certainly have some. Criminal and murderous things? No. But many regrets regarding my interactions with others, and my choices in life as a young man. I was wild and irresponsible. So the story probably came about through my meditations on my own inability to keep myself on track, for significant periods of my early life. I was in my own personal purgatory of regret. Most of my stories are metaphors for the human condition.

TDE: Based on the Great Race of Yith from Lovecraft's Cthulhu Mythos, "Broken on the Wheel of Time" is a terrific time-traveling adventure that unfurls through the journal entries of a venomous wife and husband from the late 18th century.

Obsessive, psychopathic Benjamin Berling is literally a fetid mess. "He has forgotten to shave. If a man must have a beard then let him trim it; but Ben will have none of this. His linen is unclean; he will rarely avail himself of the garments I scrub and hang for him. His odor is as sour as his disposition."

Berling cleaves to his workshop, immersed in secret study and abominable experimentation. One day, he emerges as if a new man. His wife, Gwyneth records the mystery. "A strange change has come over Ben. I should be glorying in it, since the change has wrought a softening of his temperament, but I'm almost frightened by the transformation."

As the staggering truth becomes clear, the couple's new relationship is the only defense against the impending collapse all to soon to be unleashed.

When did you hit on the idea of adding soul exchange to time travel?

JS: The story is Lovecraftian—that is something used in its Lovecraftian source. This particular story was written for my story col-

Fantastic April 1975 with Shirley's "Silent Crickets." Cover by Stephen Fabian.

Fantastic October 1978 with Shirley's "Tahiti in Terms of Squares." Cover by Steven Fabian.

lection—the only non-reprint in the book—entitled *Lovecraft Alive!* So in a true Lovecraftian story one references Lovecraftian ideas and terms and does something new with them. I took as my source story, HPL's "The Shadow Out of Time." So I cannot take credit for that idea. But I believe I've used it in a very distinctive way.

TDE: "Nodding Angel" asks the question: Are gifts of extra sensory perception part of DNA, able to pass across generations? Beth's mama has visions. She feels evil. It needles her, prompted by otherwise seemingly harmless strangers. It could mean nothing, but should the nodding angel appear above such a person, it will guide her through what must be done. Her daughter merely bears witness, until the day her own gift materializes.

What inspired this "Nodding Angel?"

JS: Of course, the nodding angel is not an angel, at all. And the seemingly harmless strangers really were. . . I just imagined a person being told to do evil by something appearing to be good . . .

TDE: In the cutthroat world of "Calaphais and the Demon Malchance," Calaphais' kindness is an anomaly. A deviant behavior certain to catch the eye of an intangible demon such as Malchance, as he whispers through the plain of men. "Malchance had three dominant peculiarities: impulsiveness, curiosity and a dislike of unpredictability in the world around him. He liked to be the very soul of unpredictability himself, but could not abide it in others." And so, Calaphais' fate was at once inevitable and sealed.

Malchance accosts the human, inflicting pain and nearly unbearable agony. Only if the wise Calaphais agrees to trick the sheiks and kings who trust him to begin a war, will Malchance release him.

Calaphais refuses and must endure more of the demon's torture. His only solace, his belief in the Beloved—something completely alien to the curious demon.

How do you choose names for your characters?

JS: The name Calaphais simply came into my mind when I was casting around for one. Malchance is a name, in translation from some language, given to him by some human sorcerer at some point, and it means what it seems to mean: bad luck personified or, from the human point of view, chaos. But Malchance also represents our worst impulses, and Calaphais represents, to me, our higher selves struggling with those impulses and finding an inner fulcrum and lever to use against the madness of Malchance through an intimate connection to the underlying light of consciousness underlying the cosmos.

TDE: "That Ambulance Again" is a short, but satisfying cyclic warp in which the victim and the offender switch places.

What do you do to help stimulate ideas for your stories, poems, and songs?

JS: I have a fairly dark, almost paranoiac turn of mind, and I exploit that to look for something that could show us the uncanny cunning of evil, or the weirdly predacious, so that we do not take the world for granted. Turning things upside down is one way to do it; it shakes us out of our complacency. And isn't that what a fan of dark fantasy and the weird wants? To be set free for a time from the restraints of the usual consensus reality? To escape the humdrum—even if it means escaping into the shadows?

The Crow screenplay by David J. Schow and John Shirley (Dimension Films, 1994)

TDE: There are four poems and the lyrics to a song interspersed through the issue that combine fantasy and horror. What can you tell us about them?

JS: As a boy I was a fan of Poe—still am, really—and that included his poetry. Also, I was into Lovecraft including his "Fungi from Yuggoth" cycle. Combine that with an interest in eerie rock and folk lyrics, from the likes of the Blue Oyster Cult, Black Sabbath, early Pink Floyd and other artists. I found the poetry of Clark Ashton Smith later in life, and was impressed, as so many others were, and also read poets like Edna St. Vincent Millay, as well as Milton and Blake. So eerie rhyming poetry is in my blood. Then along comes the S.T. Joshi journal of weird poetry—weird in the *Weird Tales* sense—*Spectral Realms*. I began to publish in that. My own emphasis is not the

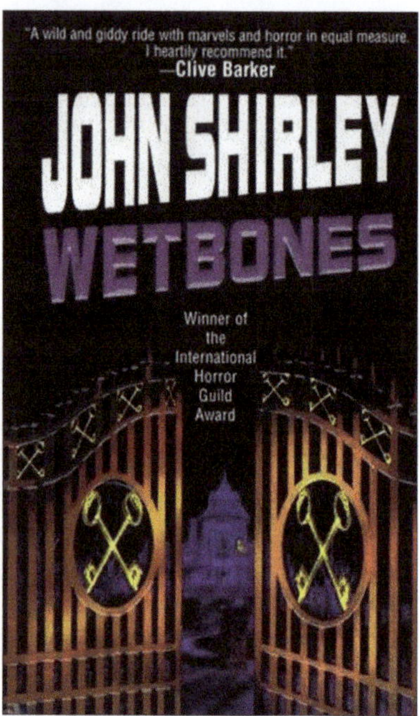

Wetbones Leisure Books, 1999

usual tropes; I try to have something definite to say, in my weird poem, and I usually am telling a story.

TDE: The novella, "Swords of Atlantis," is the cornerstone of the issue. In need of a quick payday, Snoori convinces his companion, Brimm the Savant, that treasure awaits them on Poseidonia, one of the ten kingdoms of Atlantis. "It is circled with fields and orchards and streams jumping with curious but delicious fish. And there, in an old palace, waits the beauteous Cleito, a princess who has offered ten bushels of gold to any ten men who will become the Swords of her Heart: the champions who will destroy a minor demon set in place by an addle-pated old sorcerer—a sorcerer long dead."

Seeking passage to the island, Brimm and Snoori soon find themselves manacled in a ship's bowels, shanghaied as galley slaves. The two irreverent heroes tax their wits and luck to escape one danger only to land in the midst of another. A rollicking, ricocheting adventure bordered by peril, magic, gold, and romance.

This story begs for a follow-up. Is it part of a series?

JS: While "Swords of Atlantis" is self-contained, a complete tale (with several parts) in and of itself, it is indeed also designed to be the first half of a novel, and the beginning of a series of novels. The second half has been roughly outlined. I would like to write a series of stories about Brimm and Snoori. They are an amusing duo. I wanted to write something that, while not satire or parody, still had a sense of humor. While the novella has its horrific and traditionally fantastic core, I was looking for every possible way to make the story more entertaining, and having a sense of humor about the heroes is another facet. In this I'm a bit influenced by certain Jack Vance tales, perhaps especially the Cugel stories. I grew up loving the sword and sorcery fantasy stories of Robert E Howard and Fritz Leiber, and, when I was in my early teens, Moorcock's Elric stories. I've always wanted to explore that genre in my own way and thus, here is "Swords of Atlantis." Additionally, the Atlantis story has always held a certain fascination for me. I tried to ground the novella in a reasonably real-seeming setting, as it might have been in ancient times, centuries before Anno Domini.

TDE: Describe your writing process, please.

JS: Ideas come to me readily. Most of my fiction is idea driven.

Short stories, like the ones in my issue of *Weirdbook*, are written mostly when ideas occur to me and it happens I haven't got some more demanding writing project. So then I allow them to emerge when they like, often in early afternoon. Occasionally certain kinds of stories happen when I agree to be in a themed anthology, for example one of S.T. Joshi's Lovecraftian anthologies, and I haven't got a lot on right then. I just write it at whatever time of day I feel like it. Novels, especially those I'm contracted to write, are written to some sort of schedule. I usually start around 11:30 in the morning (I have no day job, I'm a self supporting author), often re-reading and revising what I wrote the day before, then using that as a springboard, to write at least 1500 words more. I do a good deal of revision, which often involves cutting. The hardest part comes when I've been a day or two or more without writing. It then becomes hard to get started again, as writing requires a particular mental state from me which I can only describe as the flow of the writing state. Visualizing the scene, as if seeing the setting and action of a movie, help me to get started. If I'm stuck I write whatever comes to mind that could apply to the scene—and often cut that opening later. I just needed it to get started. Well, you asked . . . . I also work on poetry and lyrics. Besides writing for my own hard-rock band, The Screaming Geezers <screaming-geezers.com>, I write lyrics for the Blue Oyster Cult. None of their big hits, that was before my time. But I wrote most of the lyrics on the albums *Heaven Forbid* and *Curse of the Hidden Mirror* and on five songs on the new Blue Oyster Cult album coming in September.

TDE: Tell us about your works in progress, as of March 2020.

JS: I'm doing the umpteenth revision of my novel *Stormland* for Blackstone books—supposedly it's going to come out next year, 2021, but with the coronavirus impact on business—and publishing is a business—one wonders. It's a science fiction novel in which the meteorological extremes of climate change have created a zone of the USA in which there are hurricane-level storms 24/7 365 days a year, year after year. Why would anyone live there? Few do. Those who do have their own curious reasons. Meanwhile an investigator comes to this grim, dangerous place, following up on a cold-case serial killer and discovers a much bigger, much wilder plot involving mind control horrors. Cyberpunk/climate-fiction. He falls in with a most-peculiar "buddy" who helps him get to the horrendous and rather allegorical truth . . .

TDE: What's the best way for readers to keep up with you?

JS: Probably at <john-shirley.com/blog> there's a link there to the authorized John Shirley website. I'm no longer on facebook . . . I swore it off . . .

TDE: Thank you, John!

If you're not already a fan of *Weirdbook*, John Shirley's special edition will likely make you one. Highly recommended for fans of sword and sorcery, and horror fiction.

SCIENCE STO
HOCUS
POCUS
UNIVERSE
By Jack
Williamson

Science Stories

Article by Richard Krauss

"Either S. J. Byrne was a house name, or I was Richard Shaver ghost writing for Ray Palmer, or Ray Palmer himself, or just plain a ghost. Actually, some faces turned pale when I was introduced [at the Tenth World Science-Fiction Convention in Chicago]."
–People Who Make *Other Worlds* No. 13 from *Other Worlds* May 1953

Introduction

After an impressive run of 31 issues, *Other Worlds* came to a stop in July 1953. If Ray Palmer (1910–1977) was anything, he was a master huckster; like a seasoned HR manager able to spin benefit cuts into a gain. In hindsight, his June 1953 editorial was a plea to stick with him. "Every time you put up 35¢ for this magazine, you'll be buying a first-class ticket to adventure, entertainment and inspiration in OTHER WORLDS far beyond the imagination of yesterday, or even of today. The very fact that you are reading this means we won this month's competition. You'd be smart to remember the name OTHER WORLDS and stick with a winner!"

Well, it didn't work. Clark Publishing was in debt to their printer. Rather than continue, Palmer sold his interests in Clark to his partner, Curtis Fuller. This put the more profitable *Fate* magazine completely under the control of Curtis and Mary Fuller. They also assumed *Other World*'s debt, freeing Palmer from the obligation. The fact that a Chicago businessman was ready to invest in a new science fiction magazine didn't hurt either. Before Clark ended *Other Worlds*, Palmer had already launched Bell Publishing's first title: *Universe Science Fiction*; its first issue dated June 1953.

Then, in October 1953, *Other*

Science Stories No. 1 October 1953. Cover by Hannes Bok.

Worlds in effect became *Science Stories*, pulled from the former's full title that last appeared on *Other Worlds Science Stories* a year earlier (Oct. 1952). Palmer made the change so quickly he didn't even mention it until December, in the second issue. "The first issue was tossed in your lap with little or no ceremony, and even less explanation. For a variety of reasons—and let's be honest, most of them were financial—we had to make a spur-of-the-moment decision to discontinue OTHER WORLDS and replace it with the magazine you are now reading. We phoned the typesetter, halted work on the August OW, and lifted the editorial and stories we needed for SCIENCE STORIES No. 1 from OW material on hand."

The new digest maintained *OW*'s 35¢ price point, but went from 164 to 132 pages (counting covers); the page cut helping its financials. Palmer and Bea Mahaffey (1928–1987) continued as editors on its contents page. They also likely helmed the ship for *Universe*, but editing is credited under the publisher's name George Bell—at least for the first two issues. Bell was eager to invest in the early 1950s SF boom, but by the time he found his venue, the boom was busting. By the third issue of *Universe*, and the second of *Science Stories* (both Dec. 1953), Bell Publishing had been replaced by Palmer Publishing.

Universe fared better than *Science Stories*. The former ran ten issues, while the latter only four. Shortly after *Universe* ended (March 1955), Palmer incorporated it into a resurrection of *Other Worlds* in May 1955, going so far as to continue both *Universe* (No. 11)

and *OW*'s (No. 32) numbering sequence. The new *Other Worlds* continued dual numbering through No. 22 (No. 43) May 1957, when it transformed into *Flying Saucers from Other Worlds* (with alternating emphasis between "Flying Saucers" and "Other Worlds" every other issue). It continued solely with *Universe*'s numbering scheme, finally ending its run as just *Flying Saucers* (No. 30–32) in Dec. 1958.

Science Stories No. 1 Oct. 1953
132 pages 35¢

Like the earlier *Other Worlds*, *Science Stories* begins with "The People Who Write [Other Worlds] Science Stories" on the inside front cover. Before his biographical sketch, Jack Williamson (1908–2006) explains his cover story's origin, "One day last fall I had a pleasant surprise. A letter from Bea Mahaffey. She enclosed a photostat of a [Hannes] Bok cover painting and asked me to write a story about it. One story idea in my files seemed to fit the picture."

Hocus Pocus Universe by Jack Williamson, art by Hannes Bok

High School science teacher Charley Guilborn becomes embroiled with two of his students. Attracted to Carol Wakeman, jealous of misfit Eon Hunter, his desires are subverted by Carol's adoration of Eon. The beautiful girl poses for the boy's painting, which his father shares on a visit Charley makes to the boy's parents about his failing grades. (The same painting that graces the issue's cover.)

Frustrated in this tangled, taboo love triangle, Charley returns to school himself for his doctorate under the wing of Dr. Zerlinger, a bril-

7

Hannes Bok's illustration of Eon Hunter from *Science Stories* No. 1 October 1953.

liant scientist and leading researcher of atomic fusion. Upon graduation, Charley's invited to join Zerlinger on the secret Project Lightyear, an effort to thwart the rising Soviet threat of trans-oceanic rockets.

As Project Lightyear progresses, Carol and Eon reappear. Carol's feelings for Charley still resonate, yet she retains her unwavering belief in Eon's unorthodox notions. His greatest being his belief that belief alone will become reality.

The story fictionalizes an interesting premise we've all wondered about: How much can belief affect

A splashpanel from the *Beyond Mars* Sunday comic strip by Jack Williamson and Lee Elias.

reality? Although the question has nothing to do with the cover painting, Williamson does a good job integrating it into the story. Hannes Bok also drew a beautiful full page illustration of Eon Hunter rising through the clouds for the story's opening spread.

A prolific writer, Williamson wrote novels as well as short stories. He collaborated with Frederik Pohl on more than a dozen novels from 1954 into the 1990s. One of Williamson's early solo efforts came to the attention of Ana Barker, editor of *The New York Daily News*, via a *New York Times* review that it "ranks only slightly above that of a comic strip adventure." Barker promptly paired Williamson with artist Lee Elias for a new *Daily News Sunday* comic strip called *Beyond Mars*. The full-page feature debuted on February 17, 1952 and ran until May 13, 1955. The series was based loosely on Williamson's Seetee novels. In 1987, the comics were reprinted in two collections by Blackthorne, and in 2015 an oversized hardcover from IDW Publishing featured all 161 episodes.

Wise Guy by R.J. McGregor, art by Michael Becker

The Galaxy Survey Academy instills discipline in its cadets. "Every Galaxy Grad has been taught a thousand different ways to obey small regulations; knows why; has passed the toughest psycho-screening known to man's universe. But occasionally one slips through." Case in point: Bill Hawk, the titular wise guy.

As base disciplinarian, it's Captain Carl Klose's job to ensure compliance with Academy doctrine. Every base has one, but they operate incognito. "When you get a wise guy, you give him a chance. . . . We call it Military Functional Psychology, and it dates back a million years. The misfit fits for the good of all—or dies. Some of our failures even get medals. All die 'in line of duty' for home consumption, . . ."

Klose pulls Hawk from his weekend leave to join him on a bogus mission out on Clovis VI. His real purpose: give Hawk three chances to succeed. Follow the rules and earn your keep. Break them and die.

McGregor's portrayal of wise guy Hawk is spot on. Not a likable character, but as the tension builds, you can't help hope he'll turn things around before he's cooked.

Flight to Utopia by Jan Tourneau, art by Charles Hornstein

En route to a far away planet to begin a new colony, we join a massive astral space craft ten years into its multi-generational journey. Even its space-born toddlers won't live to see the day of their journey's end. Tourneau explores the tension between those dedicated to the mission and those who regret their decision to join, ten years out.

This appears to be Tourneau's only science fiction story.

Battle in the Sky by Robert Moore Williams, art by J. Allen St. John

Back in 1953, when every planet in the solar system supported life, Saturn's despicable—but advanced—Tethanni decide to invade Venus. They cleverly build their base of operations underground, beneath an Earth settlement. The Tethanni leader, Nevvi, gloats to Earth's Colonel John Huber, "To bomb us, you would have to kill your own people."

Huber enlists the aid of Hathor, a twenty-foot-long Venusian snake with telepathic and transcendent mental abilities to fight back. Good thing Hathor is on Earth's side.

"Battle in the Sky" hasn't aged well, but the Huber/Hathor exchanges and teamwork helped keep the story readable. Plus, it's graced with two wonderful illustrations by J. Allen St. John.

Robert Moore Williams (1907–1977) was a prolific science fiction writer whose stories appeared in *Astounding, Startling Stories*, and many other pulps. He also wrote under the names John S. Browning, H.H. Harmon, and Russell Storm. His series characters include Jongor and Zanthar. In his biographical sketch on the inside back cover, Williams says he also writes Westerns.

Pariah by Rog Phillips, art by Charles Hornstein

The best story in the issue, "Pariah," takes the honors over "Hocus Pocus," the issue's other contender. Phillips does a good job of avoiding the details that make Mary and John fugitives from the rest of society, hiding in the woods and stealing produce from farm fields to survive.

"The back door opened as they reached the top step. A man stuck his head out. 'Howdy fo—' His greeting snapped off like a light. His face did things. He swam backward through the air, leaped backward, stumbled backward—all in the same movement. He bumped the door, which then banged the kitchen wall so hard the glass window in it broke."

Roger Phillips Graham (1909–1966) was a fan and a pro. His short stories often appeared in *Amazing Stories* and *Fantastic Adventures*. His fanzine and fan activities column, "The Club House," ran in *Amazing Stories* from 1948 to 1953, and was revived for *Universe* No. 6–10.

Personals

A page and a half of short announcements for fanzines and collectors. Besides their nostalgic value one is particularly notable:

". . . SCIENCE FANTASY BULLETIN: monthly; 15¢, 12

Science Stories No. 2 December 1953. Cover by Virgil Finlay.

issues and Annual for $1.50; Harlan Ellison, 12701 Shaker Blvd, Apt. 616, Cleveland 20, Ohio; mimeographed; 40 to 50 pages of fiction, articles, poetry and features by prominent fans and pros . . ."

Science Stories No. 2 Dec. 1953
132 pages 35¢

"People Who Write" spotlights Edward Wellen, who joined a fuel company after high school, and served in World War II in the Chemical Warfare Service. After the war he wrote ad copy, and began his career as a science fiction writer with stories for *Galaxy*, *Imagination*, and *Science Stories*. By the late 1950s, Wellen expanded to crime fiction with dozens of sales to mystery digests; most often *Mike Shayne*, *Alfred Hitchcock*, and *Ellery Queen*.

As noted in our introduction, Ray Palmer's editorial this issue addresses the change from *Other Worlds* to *Science Stories*. The page cut necessitated the need to focus on stories; thus ancillary features like letters and personals would only appear if space was available. He also reports, he'd bought a half-interest in *Universe* from Bell Publications and notes his name and Bea Mahaffey's name would appear on the masthead as of issue No. 3. The other piece of big news, "we're bringing out a new magazine called *Mystic*. It's not science-fiction, but you may be interested in it because it contains stories of fantasy and occult classification, written by some of your favorite authors—Rog Phillips, Hal Annas, Randall Garrett, and Chester Geier, to name a few."

Mystic began as a fiction digest, but as time went on Palmer added the type of material he would have run in *Fate* had he not sold out to his partner in that magazine. After 16 issues, *Mystic* became *Search*, a direct competitor of *Fate*.

Potential Zero by John Bloodstone, art by Virgil Finlay

If you enjoy space action/adventure yarns, this story hits the mark very well. Written as John Bloodstone, S.J. Byrne's most common pseudonym, used here likely due to Byrne's second story in the issue, written under his real name.

"Potential Zero," is featured on the cover by Virgil Finlay, with an opening illustration by him as well. The Vanyans, a race of super-beings is colonizing Mars, transforming the red planet into a habitable world with their advanced technology. The protagonist, Ray Sanders, recalls their arrival, "You all know when they landed—August 17, 1956—on the lawn of the Capitol Building in Washington D.C., shortly after eleven P.M., Eastern Standard Time. Three traditional flying saucers, complete with peripheral observation panels and the shallow dome on top."

To say the Vanyans are benevolent is an understatement. Despite their vast superiority to humans, they happily share their advanced technology with their new neighbors. Public reaction is thankful, but skeptical. Surely these Vanyans have an underlying motive yet to be revealed. What's in this one-way exchange for them?

As the story opens, Earthly suspicions have already manifest in deadly consequence. The Vanyans have been destroyed, and the President wants to ensure his supporters continue to rejoice. Only Ray Sanders, the single Earthman to live among the Vanyans on Mars long enough to learn their language, can refute the propaganda. He fell in love with angelic Kria and traveled with her to Mars, where they were wed.

Only Sanders and Kria escaped Mars, as the Earth's attack on the planet decimated the Vanyans' encampment. They imprisoned Sanders as a traitor, and Kria, nearly killed in an assault, convalesces in a secure medical facility.

Did the Vanyans conceal deadly secrets? The President believes he has the proof after Kria's medical examination reveals her inhuman physiology. He compels Sanders to tell his story on the promise of gaining access to visit Kria one last time before his execution. The President believes he can cement public support with the release of Sander's account, followed by a revelation of the Vanyans' true nature.

The bulk of story is Sanders' report, capped in present tense by the climax and denouement. Although the "big reveal" is dated when read in 2020, the balance of the story is as engaging as Bloodstone's (Byrne's) imaginative writing:

"A description of this setting would not be complete without mention of the sleth, *a three foot, silvery globe that accompanied us, floating through the air and guided by a small box of controls and electronic gear attached to my waist. The Vanyans were addicted to moods as many Earthmen are to a graceful indulgence of alcoholics. They could not be happy for very long without music. The* sleth *was a floating portable radio, of sorts,*

but which filled the surrounding area with three-dimensional music. The symphonic notes seemed to emanate from everywhere, until you felt you were a part of them. After due adjustment to the effects of a sleth, *you ceased hearing the music, and there was only the mood—like a subtle addition to your personality. It was like feeling 'high.' but infinitely refined in its subtleties."*

In the reboot of *Other Worlds*, Ray Palmer wrote of a Byrne novel called *Tarzan on Mars*. Palmer wanted to run it, but it remained unpublished, as the Edgar Rice Burroughs estate never authorized it. (A copy of the 1954 manuscript was for sale for $500 on eBay as of Jan. 2020.)

Root of Evil by Edward Wellen, art by Michael Becker

A certified student of average intelligence seeks to enhance his mental aptitude and capacity with a hair-brained scheme involving turnips. The story ends badly—literally and figuratively.

The Bridge by S.G. Byrne, art by Charles Hornstein

Combined with "Potential Zero," S.G. Byrne's work accounts for 63% of this issue's 132 pages. "The Bridge" centers on the internal and external conflicts of Stanley Liddel, World Leader. His reign is threatened by a fragile alliance between his son and his wife that dawns on him as he recovers from a head wound inflicted by a would-be assassin. There's plenty of time between the vying of forces for Byrne to explore the desire to rule and purpose of ruling:

"Ordinary dictators gener-

ally had a Messiah complex, believing they were actually born to bring a great gift to the world, that the tyrannical measures they used were only a means to an end—an end which would be a Utopia of prosperity and freedom one day."

And

"Man's purpose was to progress, in freedom and forever, like the smallest seeds in the ground or like the immeasurable galaxies of Creation, from finite to infinite. . . . Freedom. Self-determination. The divine right to utilize the miracle of the mind with that individuality of purpose and desire which begat originality and invention—not the mass constriction into a mold that would but reflect the philosophy of one man or of one privileged group."

To raise the stakes higher, Byrne introduces a higher-level threat, a supreme alien race whose goal is to control the universe just as Liddel's son and wife wish to dominate the Earth.

Like in the earlier "Potential," Byrne saves a few twists and revelations for the end, and turns in another enjoyable escapist adventure, sprinkled with cosmic, pulpish wisdom.

Quarterback Sneak by T.P. Caravan, art by Charles Hornstein

Charles Carroll Muñoz (1926–2018) writing as T.P. Caravan, contributed primarily to Palmer's SF digests in the 1950s, along with a handful of sales to *F&SF* in the 1960s. His John & the Evil Professor series appeared in *Other Worlds*, *Universe*, and once in *Science Stories*. If "Quarterback Sneak" is representative, I'm amazed Palmer

continued to fund it. The humor is lame and the footballer stereotyping offensive. The best thing I can say about this story is that it's short—just not short enough.

She was Sitting in the Dark by Richard Dorot, art by Charles Hornstein

This story had elements of success, but overall it didn't hang together well and I felt no investment in its characters. A solo-flying spaceman's craft is swept up in a turbulent wind spout and forced to land on Gorelle—a planet thought to be uninhabited. Instead, Sam Baynes discovers a manipulative amazon, Anor, in an underground cavern, who casts an amorous spell over him, urging him to destroy her slumbering slaver, Alfdar.

Richard Shaver (1907–1975) wrote under several pseudonyms for Palmer's pulps and digests, but apparently used Dorot only once.

Optical Illusion by Mack Reynolds, art by Michael Becker

A chance encounter between a perceptive homo sapiens and an arrogant homo superior reveals a deadly, growing threat to humankind. A short, short terror tale with the prerequisite twist ending.

Palmer was smart to end the issue with a Mack Reynolds yarn, but this moderately clever three-pager isn't enough to forget the weaker entries by Caravan and Dorot that precede it.

Science Stories No. 3 Feb. 1954 132 pages 35¢

It's great to see the artists credited along with the authors in *Science Stories*, too often in digests

Science Stories No. 3 February 1954. Cover by Albert A. Nuetzell.

of this era, they aren't. This issue's "People Who Write," might have been "People Who Paint" since it spotlights Albert A. Nuetzell (1901–1969), who painted this issue's cover. Nuetzell's day job was designing motion picture titles for studios like Fox West Coast Theaters and Pacific Title. He started painting covers for science fiction magazines at the urging of his son, who was a fanatic about the genre. When he retired, he continued to produce paperback book covers, many for his son, author Charles Nuetzel. The difference in the spelling of their last names is the extra "L" added by Albert to artistically balance the "N" of his signature on his paintings.

In his editorial, Palmer offers a $500 "prize" to any unpublished author who writes the best 10,000-word story around Nuetzell's cover, which Palmer promises to publish in the August issue. Let's assume the prize was never awarded, since the April issue was *Science Stories'* last, and nothing is mentioned in the July, Sept., or Nov. 1954 issues of *Universe*.

Last Days of Thronas by John Bloodstone, art by J. Allen St. John

Palmer's appreciation for Bloodstone is evident in his editorial, ". . . the man we think is the logical successor to the great Edgar Rice Burroughs." The cover proclaims "Thronas" as "A Brilliant 45,000-Word Novel," expanding Bloodstone/Byrne's pages from 83 in the second issue to 102 in its third.

"Thronas" is an entertaining, action adventure in which two sword-wielding civilizations vie for power and dominance. Their planets are joined via spaceflight, with passage on the Golden Ship left by an advanced race, now controlled by the owner of a mysterious gem. Interspersed with battles and swordplay, Bloodstone reveals the secret histories of his opposing clans with enough twists to nearly make your head spin. Not much is what it appears to be—sometimes with the reader as confidant—but most often not.

As in his previous tales for *Science Stories*, Bloodstone/Byrne pauses the action for momentary thoughts on the nature of power and society.

"The entire system is terribly wrong. It is wrong, and it always shall be wrong, for one major section of humanity to have all of the power and the other to have none. Overbalance of power not only leads to tyranny—the step beyond it is anarchy and dissolution. On the other hand, the healthiest social balance is to give equal rights and powers to each other."

The Technical Swain by Walt Sheldon, art by Charles Hornstein

It's love at first sight between spaceman and a new hire of the International Commission, on the transport to the moon. Johnny's technical prowess is the antithesis of his social maturity, but Margo wades patiently through his plodding maturity. A sweet little nothing of a space yarn.

Walter James Sheldon (1917–1996) wrote short stories for science fiction, detective, and western pulps and digests from 1939 to 1961. His lone novel, *The Beast*, was published in 1980 by Fawcett Gold Medal.

A Stitch in Time
by Howth Castle & T.P. Caravan, art by Michael Becker

A quack psychiatrist's scheming nephew is obsessed with time travel to ensure his racing bets will make him a winner. A search for Caravan's co-writer, Howth Castle, comes up empty save numerous results for Castle Howth. Was this another humorous concoction of Caravan's or a real writing partner?

The Treason of Joe Gates
by Ralph Sloan, art by Joseph Eberle

The White House custodian waits hours for the President's late meeting to adjourn so he can clean the oval office and go home. Unfortunately, he cleans the place a little too well. Of the issue's final trio of gag shorts, this one was the best.

Sure Thing by Frank Patton, art by H.W. McCauley

Really? Another time traveler capitalizing on knowledge of the future? At least this gadget man's inspiration includes the current science fiction magazines, providing an unexpected moment of relief from the gag.

The last page of content includes Mahaffey's Statement of Ownership, Management, and Circulation, which I always find fascinating. Except this time. Under Circulation she writes, "(This information is required from daily, weekly, semiweekly, and triweekly newspapers only.)" So we get nothing.

It's a good thing Bloodstone's epic "Thronas" accounts for most of the issue. It's an exciting adventure story with bits of space travel thrown in to qualify as science fiction. Fortunately, the balance of the pages burned on short one-note groaners are few.

Science Stories No. 4 April 1954
132 pages 35¢

Another artist is highlighted in "People Who Write." This time: Virgil Finlay (1914–1971). Quite appropriate since every story in the issue is accompanied by at least one illustration by the artist—reason enough for collectors to seek out a copy. During the late 1930s, Finlay worked for A. Merritt as a feature fiction illustrator for *The American Weekly* in New York. "I stayed there for three years, during which time I began drawing for many of the fantasy and science-fiction magazines. I did my first drawings for RAP then, and through the years have continued to work for him."

RAP himself launches an editorial rant about doomsday. "Because we are in a mood today to bring it to pass. And what we think, we ARE!" It reminds me of a local radio talk show host, more interested in gleaning heated response than making a legitimate point.

The Oceans are Wide
by Frank M. Robinson, with four illustrations by Virgil Finlay

The concept of a giant spacecraft transporting human cargo to colonize a far-flung planet is similar to Jan Tourneau's "Flight to Utopia" in issue one, but Robinson expands on the idea. The Executive order manages operations throughout the ship, led by the Director, a position of heredity. The only person more powerful is the mysterious Predict, who stays hidden at the far end of the ship in his nearly inaccessible suite.

As the story opens, the Director is on his deathbed. His immature, slight-of-build son, Matty, is seen by many in the Executive order as a poor successor. They plot to destroy him and elect his cousin, Jeremiah, the tool of his aunt Reba Saylor, and her henchmen. Matty quickly comprehends what's in store and escapes, taking refuge in the Predict's lavish quarters.

The Predict charms the boy, testing his resolve, and decides he

Science Stories No. 4 April 1954. Cover by Robert Gibson Jones.

would be right for the Directorship.

"Remember that everything you do will have to be done with an eye to the good of the ship. And you'll have problems. We'll be landing in less than twenty years. You'll have problems of colonization to deal with. And you'll find out that the privileges and honors of being a Director are pretty hollow; the worries and troubles are almost infinitely great."

The population on the long

transport is strictly regulated. Those reaching the age of sixty are terminated to make room for the newborn members of the colony. Otherwise, an unsanctioned birth must be ended. In rare instances, an illegitimate is allowed to live due to exceptional traits or abilities of use to the colony.

The Predict decides Matty's features will be doctored to disguise his identity. He'll be registered as an accepted illegitimate and placed with the Reynolds family in Hydroponics. As long as he remains in hiding the Directorship will remain open until his eighteenth birthday.

At Matty's suggestion his uncle Seth is made Acting Director until Matty comes of age.

The story progresses swiftly with romance, action, and tension, as Matty and the ship traverse the years and approach their destination, a system with two hospitable planets. Several twists in which the good of the many outweigh an individual's desires help elevate this story above a routine space adventure.

Tiger's Cage by Roger Dee, art by Virgil Finlay

An alien lands on Vega IX and makes contact with the outpost's sole explorer. "I could feel it fumbling at my mind all night and half the day before it finally fell asleep, trying to communicate with me."

Macklin calls for the abilities of a Preceptive, who arrives from First Colony. When Falkner approaches the alien, they can finally understand its message. "It's here to warn us against something else, against another alien. Something so awful I can't bear—the image—"

The follow-on alien is indeed more terrible than the first, but the spacemen are spared thanks to a sobering bit of just desserts.

Roger Dee Aycock (1914–2004) wrote as Roger Dee, contributing science fiction and fantasy stories to pulps and digests from 1949 to 1971. His first novel, *An Earth Gone Mad*, was published in 1954 by Ace.

School Days by James Causey, art by Virgil Finlay

A stock 1950s/1960s SF platitude was radiation mutation. In "School Days," the enhancement isn't physical, it's mental. The ruling Vorlas take Timmy to task for cheating in school. Not the best student, he's been reaching out telepathically to genius Marsha to ace his tests for years. But what the ruling class doesn't know: Timmy's got more mental prowess about to surface.

James Causey (1924–2003) began his career with sales to *Weird Tales* in 1943. After service in World War II he returned to writing both crime and science fiction. Stark House Press has issued a collection of three of his crime novels: *The Baby Doll Murders/Frenzy/Killer Take All*.

One Thousand Miles Up by Robert Courtney, art by Virgil Finlay

Several world powers—China, England, Italy, Russia, and the United States share a manned space station armed with atomic warheads. As the story opens Washington sends a new astronaut to relieve their last one. His secret mission is to remove the foreigners so the new Pentagon will have sole control of the arsenal, thus ensuring peace.

A clever tale of espionage

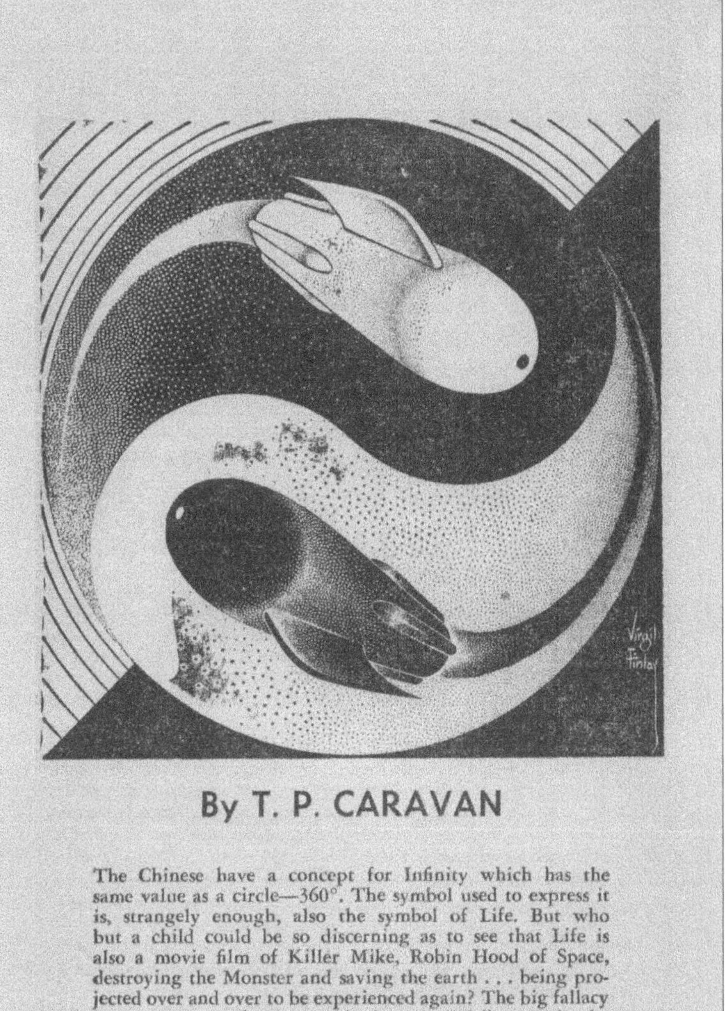

Virgil Finaly's illustration for T.P. Caravan's story in *Science Stories* No. 4 April 1954.

with enough twists to pon-
der the wisdom of the game
these countries are playing.

Robert Courtney was a pseudonym of Frank M. Robinson
(1926–2014) who began his career
in the pulps, then worked for William Hamling as an editor at *Rogue
Magazine*, and pursued many other
writing assignments, including
novels. An avid collector, his library
was one of the greatest collections of
pulps and original art ever assem-
bled. He also appeared as himself
in Gus Van Sant's movie *Milk*.

Inferiority by James Causey,
art by Virgil Finlay

Unlike a symbol of war, Causey's Mars is: "A race of artisans. Poets, artists! And no survival quotient. A race of vegetarians." Here, the beautiful and talented Avila, paid tribute to Marl Jedsen, an Earthman, carving a perfect likeness of him in topaz. But when he betrayed her, leaving the planet without a word, she destroyed it.

Five years later, when Marl returns, Avila can't help her feelings for him resurface. But this time she resolves to write a new ending.

Problem in Geometry
by T.P. Caravan, art by Virgil Finlay

Wendy Bousfield wrote about Finlay's art in *Science Fiction, Fantasy, and Weird Fiction Magazines* (Greenwood Press, 1985): *"His finest drawing* [in this issue] *illustrates T. P. Caravan's "Problems in Geometry": the yang and yin in the form of two spaceships. While Finaly's drawings are consistently far more impressive than the stories that he illustrates for SS, Finlay does not go outside the world the author has created for his images."*

There's a humorous thread running through this story, but it balances acceptably well, making this Caravan's best story in *SS*. The drama: a crisis erupts aboard a space ferry as their computor is blown apart at the hands of an extremist saboteur. The humor: a young crewman's obsession with Killer Mike, adventure hero, has him watching film reels of his hero's exploits on a continuous loop. An idea that triggers a solution to the crew's navigation problem with the loss of their computor.

The Secret of Pierre Cotreau
by Frank Patton, art by Virgil Finlay

What irony that the final story of this digest's series is also its worst. Despite its status as the cover story and its beautiful interior art by Finlay, "Secret" is a waste of space and ink. Perhaps in 1954 someone thought a stereotyped French lumberjack kidnapping a beautiful alien woman to beat, rape, and enslave would make a funny premise for a goofy story. Even the cover is tainted, once you know the story behind it. And wouldn't you know, Frank Patton was another pseudonym used by both Richard Shaver and Ray Palmer.

Summary

Despite its terrible final note, there are still reasons collector's should consider *Science Stories* worthy of pursuit. First, it's part of the *Other Worlds* run, thinly disguised behind its predecessor's subtitle. Second, the short novels or novelettes that lead each issue are good, solid space adventures worth reading for those who appreciate escapist fiction. Third, the artwork. Kudos to Palmer and Mahaffey for buying art and crediting their top-flight artists for every story in the run.

References
Al Nuetzell Webpage
Galactic Central
Internet Speculative Fiction Database
Science Fiction, Fantasy, and Weird Fiction Magazines edited by Marshall B. Tymn and Mike Ashley Greenwood Press, 1985
Transformations: The Story of the Science-Fiction Magazines from 1950 to 1970 by Mike Ashley Liverpool University Press, 2005
Wikipedia

ACTIVELY BUYING

High prices paid. All genres wanted. One piece or lifetime collections. No collection too large or small.

ACTIVELY SELLING

Thousands of Pulps in stock. We love servicing your want lists. Items added to our website weekly.

www.FantasyIllustrated.net

DEALING SINCE 1969

Prompt professional service. Specializing in Pulp magazines and science fiction/fantasy/horror first editions. Vintage paperbacks and comic books.

Contact DAVE SMITH

(425) 750-4513 - (360) 652-0339
rocketbat@msn.com
P.O. Box 248 Silvana, WA 98287

www.FantasyIllustrated.net

EconoClash Review No. 5

Review by Richard Krauss

Now published under the Down & Out Books brand, *ECR* continues its mission to provide quality cheap thrills to students of indie genre fiction.

Welcome Thrill Seekers

by J.D. Graves

ECR's editor and host introduces the title's gonzo sensibilities and a preview of what's in store in issue five: "We've got sci-fi/horror/noir/crime/and humor just a page turn away." Each story is categorized on the contents page and opens with an illustration by Duane Crockett.

California Communion (Sci-Fi)

by Cynthia Ward

Take a character so indelibly drawn, he remains entrenched in his own idiosyncratic bent no matter what comes his way. Add a sobering incident and watch the fireworks. Case in point: an extraterrestrial encounter with a surfer dude peeing into the wind.

Silo (Sci-Fi) by Cameron Mount

Infrastructure maintenance is overdue on many roadways and public facilities. So what makes you think the same is not true deep in the bowels of a missile silo? But LT James Simmons has enough workarounds to keep the aging equipment working. Everything's fine until an unwanted visitor shows up for launch.

Mr. Muffin (Noir) by E.F. Sweetman

A nameless PI, under the pseudo-tutelage of Bud Nowak of Alliance Investigations, volunteers to recover a stolen cat. First stop, the client's house. "Rudy answered the door looking like a shut-in. He was pale and squishy, with long greasy hair, dressed in a stained tee shirt and baggy sweat pants."

Mr. Muffin, the Persian cat, was stolen by a prostitute named Shayla, who had visited Rudy at the house during a few hours of the day when his mother was out. As the investigation proceeds, the PI begins to wonder if this was a kidnapping or a rescue.

The Retcon (Sci-Fi)

by R. Daniel Lester

Writing dictums advise writers to start in *medias res*. Lester does that in spades. But the landscape here is invented, so it takes a few pages to recoup equilibrium. Once you catch onto things, this tech noir delivers the prerequisite thrills and downers.

Luck Be a Bullet (Crime)

by Aeryn Rudel

A successful bounty hunter neglects a single basic bit of research that nearly costs him the farm. This Ukrainian mob-infused standoff strikes just the right balance of gravity and levity.

The Bridesmaid (Crime)

by David Rachels

A smart follow-on to the previous story, "Bridesmaid" puts the emphasis on humor over its somber mobster setting. Lucien Legrand wants to be a hitman, but aside from his lack of research, planning, and secrecy, he can't hit a target a social distance away. So what happens when you miss a hit?

Hell Yeah! (Horror) by Die Booth

A trio of high school goof-balls tire of their usual pranks and try their luck with a ouija board. Just as their cleverness wears out something unexpected turns up. The demon, Urnan, and he's ready to sit for a spell.

Service with a Smile (Transgressive/Noir) by Adam S. Furman

A seriously grungy private eye, Jake Timberpott, prods a court messenger to tag along on a skip-trace to deliver a petition. It's definitely the journey not the destination as Judge Hanneghan's messenger, Randall, gets way more street lessons than he bargained for.

"I think he broke my leg."

"If you can whine, it means you're fine." Jake chuckled. "My dad always used to tell me that. Now I see what he meant."

The Sleep-Tights (Horror) by Aristo Couvaras

If sleep deprivation goes on long enough, it'll kill you. But what if sleep itself was deadly? That's the conundrum facing Doug, Candace, Megan, and everybody else when alien invaders disintegrate anyone who falls asleep. An outré concept that Couvaras pulls off remarkably well.

Aid and Comfort (Transgressive/Sci-Fi) by J. Manfred Weichsel

After thwarting the invasion of Rillians, life on Earth returns to near-normal. Except for the foot soldiers the Rillians abandoned

EconoClash Review No. 5. Cover by Eric Asaris.

when they fled. Those are left to be picked off by the authorities whenever they rear their froggy heads. But when uber PC Dad welcomes Jak into his home to teach his children tolerance through example, he gets a lesson of his own.

The issue wraps up with author bios that list other works and websites. And there are numerous full-page ads for other indie novels and digest collections for those looking for good companions to *ECR*.

EconoClash Review, *Switchblade*, and *Pulp Modern* continue to showcase the best of hard-wrought indie genre fiction. This issue of *ECR* delivers another crusty collection of ten terse tales guaranteed to divert, debauch, and delight.

Sock Monster

Crime fiction by Rick Ollerman
Illustration by Michael Neno

"... it all felt so wrong until he finally realized she was up to something."

It made sense to him, then, back when it started. He thought it was when she had taken a pair of his boxers from the wet pile he'd left on top of one of the dryers. He never actually saw her take them, he wasn't even in the room when they'd disappeared, but he did see her looking at him in that way, that peculiar knowing way. That was her first mistake: she had made herself stand out. And that was when he knew his life was about to change.

The immediate problem was that he needed figure out what to do about it. Although they lived

in the same four story building, they weren't friends, they weren't acquaintances, and he didn't even know her name let alone which apartment she lived in. But he'd find out now. He'd have to if he were going to figure out what she was really up to.

His name was Frederick Tobey and he worked as a CPA for the Freedom General Insurance Company. They were a large concern with many holdings, all of whose taxes were filed by the staff on the sixteenth floor of their eponymous building located in lower Manhattan. Frederick Tobey rode a bus and then two subway trains to work, from Brooklyn to Manhattan, there and back, each and every week day. Tobey rarely took sick days and hadn't gone on an actual vacation since Elizabeth left him nearly fifteen years ago.

During this morning's commute, Tobey kept turning the matter of his missing boxers over and over in his mind. It didn't make sense at first but that's what made it so damned clever. The woman hadn't done anything obvious when he passed her in the hallway, she'd just given him that look, as though she couldn't help herself. But that was all he needed, he thought.

His work day was difficult; clearly he couldn't be expected to concentrate on his job with some kind of plot going on against him. Fortunately it was late in the autumn and the mayhem of tax season had passed. This meant that he could more or less cruise through the motions of his daily routine while part of his brain worked constantly on this new problem.

Was he in any danger? How could he know, he wondered. He decided he didn't have enough facts yet and he asked his supervisor if he could go home an hour or so early. Given the light work load of the time of year this was not an uncommon request for the rest of the staff but coming from Fred Tobey, who never took time off, it was most remarkable, and raised a few eyebrows. But it wasn't a problem and Tobey left the office at three o'clock. No one noticed his passage.

During the long subway commute Tobey knew he had to take a few risks in order to safeguard his own future. He'd begin by staking out the mail boxes in the front vestibule of the apartment building. If he could pinpoint his aggressor's apartment number, he'd at least know where she was some of the time. Perhaps he could even find out her name.

Surely she wouldn't try anything in the front vestibule, not at that time of the day, in full sunlight. If he was as careful with his facial expressions and body language as he thought he could be, she shouldn't tumble to the fact that he knew something was going on.

Last night's laundry was done on Tuesday. The next laundry time was on Friday at eight o'clock. Two days. Just two days for him to figure out what was happening around him.

While he waited just inside the glass paneled security door, Tobey thought about Elizabeth. He hadn't been so paranoid since the divorce. The way she had constantly gone through his clothes, had read all of his mail, even told him how he should drink his coffee;

it all felt so wrong until he finally realized she was up to something. He wondered at the time if the divorce had literally saved his life. And now there was this.

He wondered what Elizabeth was up to now. There hadn't been any contact since she left, which was a relief. No requests for alimony, either, which Tobey still found suspicious.

Perhaps, though, he was exaggerating. Surely there were logical, pedestrian reasons for himself and this new woman to have come together the way they have. There were over three hundred units in this building alone; surely pure statistical chance could have taken a hand and touched the two of them together.

It was in this slightly more relaxed state that he found himself when the woman finally walked through the door that faced the street. Unsuspecting, she walked directly to her mailbox, in plain sight through the security door, and opened the small bronze door with her key. Tobey couldn't make out the number from where he was but now he knew how to find the right mailbox. In a marvelous coincidence it was just two up from his own.

This meant he wouldn't have to risk another personal encounter and he quickly darted up the stairway behind him. He listened from the landing and could hear her as she called and was then swallowed up by the creaky old elevator.

Nearly grinning, he stole back down the stairway, making sure she had gone. Some of these people could be sneaky. He had married one, after all, so he knew all about them.

Standing up straight, feeling calmer now after his reflections from the stakeout, he strode into the vestibule and found the right box.

His knees went weak as he read the number. How could this be? How long has all this been going on? He walked as fast as he could away from the mail boxes and back up the stairs. He knew it wasn't rational but he wasn't going to feel safe until he made it inside his own apartment, 214.

Tobey dead bolted the door after himself and couldn't help but look upwards as he forced himself to calm down. This was no time to lose control.

She was up there now, he knew, in apartment 414. Two floors above him, directly overhead. There was something sinister about this. He staggered over to the sofa and tried to sit, but he missed and crumpled onto the floor. He lay there for hours, his head cradled in his arms, fingers enmeshed in his hair. Later, when he realized he had wet himself, he crawled across the floor to his bathroom shower.

Thursday. One more day. Tobey wanted to call in sick but he didn't dare do anything so obvious. The last thing he could afford to do was tip his hand, to let them know that he was on to them. As long as they didn't have a clue he could act with some freedom and control.

In the office he set about filling his day with meaningless meetings. He scheduled them via e-mail and the network calendar programs. No matter what else happened, he wanted to leave a trail and document his day as much as possible. If something were to happen to Frederick Tobey by god he'd have left his mark. Strength in the face of adversity. There would be a trace of him left behind.

By the time he got home, he was exhausted. His mind kept turning back to the missing boxing shorts. Why had the woman in 414 taken that particular pair? What made them different from any others?

The next thought hit him with an icy wave as he fumbled with the boiling water and his tea. Elizabeth? Could 414 be working with his ex-wife? Again, though, for what reason? But Elizabeth did know his clothes, and she'd know he wouldn't change all that much in twelve years.

Too much, too much, too much, he told himself as he began to slip to the floor. *NO! Keep it together, god damn it!* He wasn't sure if he'd shouted out loud or not but he was very nearly past caring.

Tobey took several deep breaths and tried to visualize calming things. He tried ocean waves but the sounds of the crashing surf were too distracting. He tried brilliant white cumulus clouds slowly floating through a bluer than blue sky as he laid on his back in an open field of rich green grass. But the blades made his back itch and he couldn't be still. Plus there were ants. He pictured himself floating on his back in a wide, shallow pool, his body barely breaking the water's surface and not wanting to sink, bobbing gently at the surface. Slowly, though, tiny streams of water trickled into his ears and made him twitch uncomfortably.

Although he was still hugging his knees to his chest on the floor of his kitchen, things were better, more settled. Just to be sure, he checked himself and his pants were dry. Not wanting to upset things again, he crawled his way across the floor and into his bathroom.

Fighting hard to retain his fragile equilibrium (but *Elizabeth!*), he swallowed a small white pill from a glassine bag with a zippered top. It was supposed to be a generic Ambien that he purchased over the internet. The web site was from Canada but the shipping label said the package had come from Texas. Tobey thought this meant the pills themselves may have come across the Mexican border but he didn't really care. He'd always trusted the mailman.

Regardless of what the pill was, it helped him get to sleep if he took it and didn't try to stay awake. And he never had to submit to a doctor or get stuck with a needle or hit with a hammer or prodded with a finger.

He fell asleep in his bath tub, curled into a ball and dreaming of conspiracies. But thanks to the pill, whatever it was, all of it would be beyond his memory when he awoke.

Now it was Friday and Tobey was refreshed and alert. He almost felt good, he thought, until he realized where he was. Picking himself out of the tub, he walked into his bedroom and peeled off the clothes he had slept in, throwing them into the wicker laundry basket Elizabeth had bought for them when they'd originally taken the apartment.

Laundry. Elizabeth. Tonight…
Laundry night.

Tobey felt much more calm in the morning. It was as if he had an internal reset that could be pushed overnight, allowing him to pick up his life at the beginning of every day and move on.

He shaved, showered and breakfasted, absolutely determined to carry on a normal day. Just as he did yesterday, he'd remain calm and predictable to a fault. Whatever was going on with 414, with or without his ex-wife, would unravel in its own good time. At least that's what he told himself over and over again during his commute.

At work before lunch it was much the same as the day before. Scheduled meeting after scheduled meeting, Tobey imprinted his mark upon the work lives of those around him. No matter what happened, these people would remember Frederick Tobey.

Things grew darker around lunch time, however. Being the off season, his co-workers began to leave on a kind of semi-sanctioned early weekend. Tobey nearly panicked. What if he were left alone at work, exposed, with no one able to vouch for his movements? Or keep him safe?

He himself left at noon for a cup of coffee at the deli across the street. He didn't feel up to solid food and he was right. After two sips of coffee he ran to the rest room and vomited repeatedly into the stinking toilet. When he was through he nearly ran out the door.

According to his watch it wasn't even twelve thirty. Too early to go back to the office. Maybe a walk would help.

Tobey headed east into the afternoon sunlight, visible in patches high above the Manhattan skyline. After half a block he began to shiver.

Turning abruptly, Tobey careened off the shoulders of half a dozen pedestrians before being able to right himself and plot a course back along the way he had come.

His fingernails and lips nearly blue, and with a full on case of teeth chattering chills, he fought his way back to the lobby of his building. Pacing back and forth along the bank of windows, he gradually began to feel warm again. It was seventy six degrees outside.

He returned to the sixteenth floor and found it nearly deserted. What the hell would he do now, he wondered. It wasn't unheard of for the staff to be granted an unofficial half day during an especially pleasant off season fall day, but would it really be likely to happen this week? The same week a particular pair of his boxer shorts were stolen by a strange woman who just *happened* to live in the apartment TWO FLOORS DIRECTLY OVERHEAD? It strained credulity. He decided he wasn't going anywhere.

Tobey found the department's clerk; he was an older man, semi-retired, and management simply never thought to extend the same privileges to him as the rest of the staff. What a perfect alibi, Tobey thought.

Throughout the tax season, pile after pile of manila folders, report binders, and other miscellaneous paperwork would accumulate until some point late in the year when "volunteer" pizza parties were held over a weekend. The staff would come dressed in jeans and t-shirts, munch pizza, tell stories and mindlessly file things.

This was what Tobey needed and he set about the task with a maniacal efficiency. At one point it occurred to him that the work was like lifting weights. Requiring no intellectual thought, the exertion nevertheless induced a focus so sharp all other thoughts were obliterated. Running or walking didn't work this way, he knew; he had been on his cross country running team in high school. When running, the last thing you can do is get away from your own thoughts, no matter how much you may want to.

The clerk had to remind him when it was time to go. Five o'clock and he had his own mass transit timetable to keep.

Fine, Tobey thought. At least he'd made it this far in the day on his own terms.

But that still left tonight.

All the way home and all through his dinner Tobey considered things as rationally as he could. While he still didn't know exactly what it was they were up to, he had identified at least one of the people against him. But they had the advantage of time, he thought; the wheels of their plot had likely been turning since well before last Tuesday when his shorts were taken. After all, 414 couldn't have just moved in, exactly two floors above Tobey, Tuesday afternoon in time to rendezvous with his laundry. That would be crazy.

The most important thing he'd done, he thought, was not tip his hand. He may not know much about 414, or her possible connection with Elizabeth, or any of the rest of it, but he was reasonably sure they didn't know he knew something bad was happening, that something was really wrong.

At seven forty five, slowly and deliberately, he collected all of tonight's laundry in his ancient wicker basket. He didn't know what else to do but forge ahead with his routine. He didn't want to tip them

off and he certainly didn't want to play sitting duck all alone in his apartment waiting for god knew what to happen. He put his plastic bottle of detergent on the top, along with his fabric softener, and at five minutes to eight left his apartment.

Sometimes he took the stairs down to the first floor, but not usually. He didn't want to risk finding himself alone in the elevator with one of his opponents, at least not on this particular night, so he decided to risk the walk. It wasn't such a big break in his routine and if he were lucky, no one would notice. He seemed to have been lucky enough so far.

Once Tobey made the laundry room without incident, he nodded to a woman he knew as a Mrs. McAdams who had just finished loading the complex's two dryers. She said good evening and squeezed out the door, her plastic basket squished against her side.

This was okay, thought Tobey. Mrs. McAdams had lived in the building longer than he had so it was unlikely she was part of the plot. Since the dryer cycles ran longer than the washers', though, his own clothes were going to have to wait their turn again. But wait—that was just like last Tuesday.

With a trickle of sweat working its way down the back of Tobey's neck, he fed his clothes into the two waiting washers. One for dark, the other for whites. Now that he'd committed to maintaining his normal routine, he couldn't shake the feeling that he was somehow becoming as much a spectator as well as a participant. It was a strange feeling.

When the sweating grew worse and he began to shake, he checked his watch and went back to his apartment. He'd be back in eighteen minutes, the same as always. No sir, nothing unusual going on here.

Except for a dedicated and manic pacing in Frederick Tobey's living room, nothing out of the ordinary happened. At the appropriate time, he returned to the laundry room and calmly and efficiently transferred his damp clothing from the spent washers to the tops of the two front loading dryers.

This was just the way he did it last Tuesday, the way he always did it. He managed an enforced sort of calm by screaming a melody from some long dead composer, Mahler, he thought, in his mind. He projected the same snippet over and over and over, his movements unconsciously falling into time with the music in his head.

And then it was back upstairs for another twelve minutes. But now he had the dryers reserved. And, he wondered, if a new move was underway, if a new die had been cast, something would happen soon. The music crescendoed in his head.

Precisely twelve minutes later, Tobey was back. Mrs. McAdams had just completed the transfer of her own laundry back to her basket for the trip back to her apartment, number 109, to be folded in front of the television set, comfortable in her own routine.

Tobey said goodnight, loaded the two dryers, and with a deep sense of dread trudged back upstairs. He had another forty minutes to wait and by now the music in his head had finally stopped playing. It no longer helped.

Inside fifty minutes Tobey was back inside his apartment, no problems, no woman from 414, nothing unusual. As he shot the dead bolt on the door he dropped to his knees and began gulping air like a giant beached fish, his laundry basket crushed in front of him in a two-handed death grip.

When he felt his body wouldn't betray him if he moved, he crawled over to the center of his living room, dragging the basket behind him.

Folding time. Then he could relax, he thought, perhaps mix himself a cocktail. He had survived something, he thought, even if he didn't quite know what it was.

The droning of the television and the calming of his euphoria almost made him miss it. Tobey sat bolt upright and went through the neatly folded piles again. And then again.

They had made their move after all.

How could he have been so stupid? What chance did he have, trying his best to behave normally, performing so well at his job, being such a good person, all the while thinking he could resist the people doing this? *They* held all the cards, *they* knew what this was all about. What was he to that?

He was a fool, he thought, but he wouldn't be any more. He may not be smart enough to figure out what was going on, but he could damn well play the one card he held without them being able to do anything about it. He could see to that.

Tobey flew from his apartment as fast as he could, before the fear overwhelmed him, and ran down the hall and up the two flights of stairs until he stood in front of apartment 414. Without pausing he hammered on the door with his fist, then took a cautious step back.

The door opened a foot and she was there alright, holding back the shock she must have felt at the sudden sight of her nemesis.

"Hello?" she said, sounding merely curious.

She wasn't even trying to lie, thought Tobey as he rushed the door, driving the edge of it into the woman's forehead and knocking her to the floor. She turned away from Tobey on her hands and knees and tried to stand up.

"Where are they?" Tobey bellowed. "Where are my shorts and t-shirt?"

The woman stumbled forward and Tobey could see her target, a telephone on a small table neatly positioned on a small rug at the entrance to the bedroom hallway. Without a thought he pushed her square in the back with both hands. Her feet caught on the edge of the rug as she flew forward, knocking the table over and sending the phone spinning further down the hall.

Tobey jumped on her back, driving the air from her lungs as she clawed at the floor in front of her. He wrapped his fingers in the curls of her long blonde hair and jerked her head back and then drove her face into the floor. He did this many times.

"Where are my clothes?" he yelled again and again, in time with his pounding. If he could just get them back, where would that leave them? They'd have nothing, nothing at all, and of course they wouldn't try anything again, not once they realized how he's been on to them for so long.

The woman wasn't making any more sounds. She had landed across the small area rug and the telephone cable it had been covering was under her chin. Tobey grabbed it and pulled it towards him, around the woman's neck, pulling and pulling with all the strength he had left.

Eventually he pushed himself off her back and stood up behind her, an expression of sublime triumph on his face. He could see a wetness spread through the seat of her denim jeans. "Hah!" he said to the figure on the floor. "How do you like it?"

His sense of liberation, of having been set free, was intoxicating. He staggered back toward the front door, strangely uncoordinated, when he saw the thing on her kitchen counter.

The laundry basket.

If laundry had been so important to their plan, he could think of one other way to throw them off. They have a couple of his things, but he could have their whole basket.

He snatched it from the counter and ran.

Not long after, when the knock came at the door, Tobey opened it to see two men in sport coats standing in the hall.

"Yes?" he asked, still feeling wonderful.

"Frederick Tobey?" the taller one asked.

"Of course," Tobey said. "What can I do for you?"

"We're police, Mr. Tobey. May we come in?"

Tobey stepped back as the two detectives introduced themselves and followed him inside. "Do you know a woman named Amanda Peters in apartment 414, sir?" the shorter one asked as his eyes swept across the room.

A wide grin grew across Tobey's face as he realized what this meant. This Peters woman, his ex-wife Elizabeth, they didn't get him. Their plan had been smashed to pieces and he had won. All by himself, without anyone else's help, he had beaten them. He was truly Frederick Tobey.

The taller of the two detectives gestured at the neat piles of bras, panties, and other bits of women's clothing arranged about the carpet. "Is this your laundry, sir?" he asked.

"I did good, didn't I?" said Tobey.

"Um, yes, sir. Real good," the shorter one told him. "Turn around, please, and clasp your fingers behind your head."

"She should have been more clever, I think, but she let me see her on Tuesday."

The two cops looked at each other as they attached a pair of handcuffs to Tobey's wrists. They read him his rights as they walked him out of his apartment and into the elevator but he wasn't really listening. From deep down inside, he felt too damned good for silly distractions.

Riding in the back seat of their car, halfway to wherever it was they were taking him, a sudden thought hit him like an electric shock delivered at the end of a giant sledge hammer. His euphoria evaporated with an icy chill and his stomach knotted as he fought to control his breathing and his bladder.

The boxers, he thought, and the t-shirt: where were they?

He hadn't found them.

This thing wasn't over.

But what was he to do next?

Rick Ollerman has written four novels and a collection of non-fiction. Several short stories are slated to appear this year as he works on a new novel.

Digest SF Novels

"Book-Length" Reprints of Science Fiction and Fantasy Stories

Article by Vince Nowell, Sr.

Amazing Stories Novel No. 1
20 Million Miles to Earth

This was the best place I could think of to start writing about digest-format reprint novels. Yet I begin with a novel that was not a reprint, unless you count the screenplay script as an original issue. I'm referring to Henry Slesar's *20 Million Miles to Earth*, published in digest-size soft-cover format in 1957 by Ziff Davis Publishing Co. Ostensibly it was *Amazing Stories Science Fiction Novel* No. 1, but ended up as a one-shot venture.

The book was adapted from the motion picture released in 1957 by Columbia Pictures, with special movie effects by Ray Harryhausen (a close friend to Ray Bradbury).

The book's front cover artwork is by Ed Valigursky. Strangely, Slesar's Wikipedia biography omits any credits for his adapting the movie to book form.

Columbia Publishing Co.
City of Glass by Noel Loomis

I've seen quite a few copies of this work available at paperback

---

Author's Note: This article does not cover the *Galaxy Science Fiction Novels* of the 1950s & 1960s as these were dealt with nicely by Steve Carper in *The Digest Enthusiast* No. 4.

book shows. It was a 1955 "Double-Action Pocketbook" reprinted from the July 1942 story in *Startling Stories*. It bears a color front cover and b&w back cover, both by EMSH.

Merit Books (Century Publications)

Merit produced a pair of digest-size novels in the early 1950s. The first, in 1950, was *Operation Interstellar* by George O. Smith. I cannot

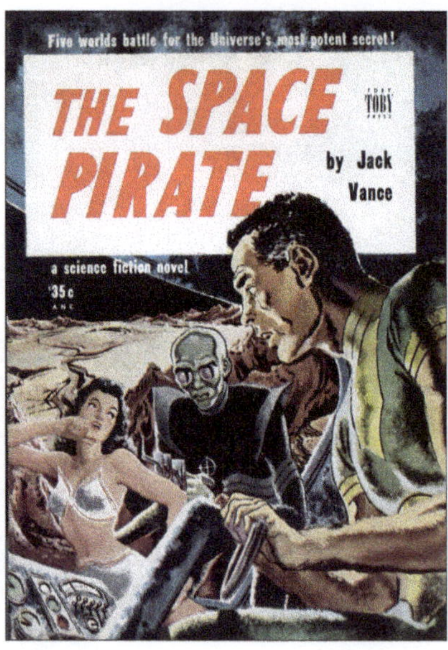

trace a prior publishing entry, and therefore I assume this was a First Edition. However, it may have been used by Ray Palmer in one of his magazines. It bears a front cover by Malcolm Smith. The second book, also possibly an original, was *World of IF* by Rog Phillips.

Prize Science Fiction Novels/ Crestwood Publishing

Prize produced a pair of digest-sized novels, almost before the onslaught of digest-sized magazines began. In 1949, Prize published Murray Leinster's *Fight For Life—A Novel of the Atomic Age.* This novella is from the March 1947 *Startling Stories,* where it was entitled "The Laws of Chance," and then reprinted in *Fantastic Story Magazine* in Spring 1954 after appearing as Prize Novel No. 10 in 1949. The second book, marked "No. 11," was *Sojarr of Titan—A Novel of the Future* by Manly Wade Wellman. This is another digest novel I found for sale

time and again. It's from the March 1941 issue of *Startling Stories.*

Toby Press

Then there is the First Edition Toby Press Science Fiction Novel *The Space Pirate—Five Worlds Battle for the Universe's Most Potent Secret!* by Jack Vance. This 1953 novel was later republished as *The Five Gold Bands.* Toby Press mostly produced psychology and self-help books and magazines.

Novels from The Most Thrilling Science Fiction Ever Told (1968–1969)

These are three "double-novel" issues produced as part of the *Most Thrilling* series of magazines put out by the Ultimate Publishing & Distributing (UPD) Company under Sol Cohen. When I was still collecting, I even shelved these with my digest-sized novels, rather than with the UPD reprint magazines. The stories were, of course, originally

long novelettes or even novellas, and all had appeared in Ziff Davis' (or later) *Amazing Stories* or some other UPD-copyright-owned magazine.

Fall 1968

Special Murray Leinster 50th Anniversary Issue, front cover art by Edward Valigursky. The editor first presents "The Golden Years: An Anniversary," a brief biography of Murray Leinster (Will F. Jenkins) who began writing fifty years before this issue. Then follow two novellas: *Long Ago and Far Away* (illustrated by Virgil Finlay) from *Amazing Stories* September 1959, and *Planet of Dread* (illustrated by Dan Adkins) from *Fantastic* May 1962. These are listed on the cover as "Two Complete Novels."

Winter 1968–69

Front cover art by Edward Valigursky. The first "novel" is *Gold In the Sky* by Alan E. Nourse from *Amazing Stories* September 1959 and

illustrated by Llewellyn. The second is *The Goddess of World 21* by Henry Slesar from *Fantastic* for March 1957, and illustrated by Virgil Finlay.

Spring 1969

Front cover art by EMSH and Virgil Finlay. The lead novel is *Kragen* by Jack Vance, a novella that ran in *Fantastic* in July 1964, and is illustrated inside by EMSH. The second is *Beacon to Elsewhere* by James H. Schmitz (both front cover and interior artwork by Virgil Finlay) from his *Amazing Stories* novella of April 1963.

The Elusive British "Look–Alikes" —An Aside

I can't think of any better place to mention the U.K.- published Nova Science Fiction Novels series. These started, then stopped, then started again in Spring 1953 to Summer 1953, and Fall-Winter 1954 to sometime in 1956.

These Galaxy Novel-like digest-

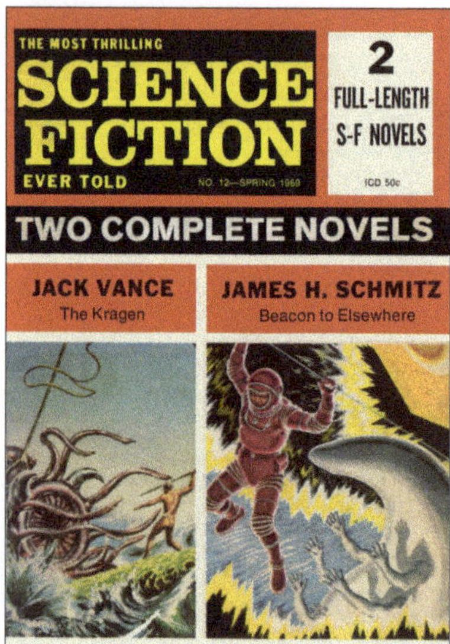

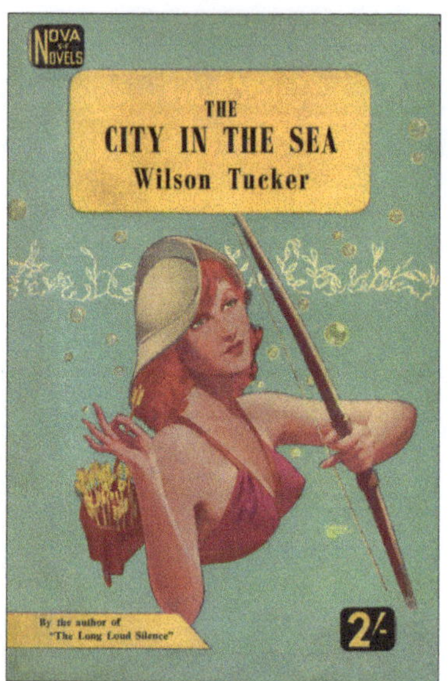

size publications were companions to *New Worlds Science Fiction* and *Science-Fantasy*. The two zines' success inspired the novels idea, but alas cheap paper and overrun costs by the printer put a major dent in the plans. Most of my information on these came from Sean Alan Wallace ("Remembering Nova Science Fiction Novels") and Brad Day's *Checklist*.

Series One: Spring 1953

Stowaway to Mars by John Beynon (Harris, aka Wyndham), front cover by Hutchings. There was supposed to be a second novel, *Ballard of the Space Patrol* by Malcolm Jameson, edited by André Norton, but apparently it was never published. So-o-o-o . . . fall back and regroup!

Series Two

(Mentioned here because I am intrigued and would like to see proof of these issues. just for ducks.) They appear online as *fait accompli*.

No. 1 (or No. 2 total) *The*

Weapon Shops of Isher by A. E. van Vogt, Fall-Winter (November) 1954.

No. 2 (or No. 3 total) *City In the Sea* by Wilson Tucker, also November 1954(?).

No. 3 (or No. 4 total) *The Dreaming Jewels* by Theodore Sturgeon, January 1955.

No. 4 (or No. 5 total) *Jack of Eagles* by James Blish, also January 1955(?).

I have heard that there are even more reprint/digest novels out there somewhere. I have no data about them, however, if they do exist. So if you are a sci-fi collector, there's an exciting *"World of the Unknown Issues"* out there somewhere just waiting for your discovery. Good luck!

Vince Nowell (Sr.), a sixth-generation native Californian, is a retired technical writer. He has been reading and collecting science fiction & fantasy since 1950.

ANC
SINGAPORE
from the
Universal-International Picture
by Seton I. Miller
CENTURY MYSTERY
25¢
COMPLETE
and
UNABRIDGED
FRED MacMURRAY and AVA GARDNER
with Roland Culver · Richard Heydn · Thomas Gomez · Spring Byington
Directed by John Brahm · Produced by Jerry Bresler
From the Screenplay by Seton I. Miller & Robert Thoeren

Photoplay Editions

Article by Steve Carper

"Photoplay Editions weren't for the mainstream book crowd; they aimed at the same readers that bought dime novels and pulp magazines by the millions."

Nothing is more predictable than the appearance of what Amazon calls a "movie tie-in edition," a novelization of a blockbuster movie. Every big franchise spawns them, from *Assassin's Creed* to *X-Men: The Dark Phoenix Saga* to bookcases full of novels set in the Star Wars and Star Trek universes. Audiences get to take their stories home, with extras: more scenes, more dialog, more explanations, and almost always stills from the movie and/or of the stars. This type of "merch" is a cheap and reliable source of extra income and extra promotion for the movie studio.

The studios have known this since forever, since before movies to novelize existed. "Stage-play editions" of Broadway productions begin to appear in 1898 when Sarony/H. M. Caldwell released a prose adaptation of J. M. Barrie's *The Little Minister*, complete with stills from the play, setting the template every other publisher would follow.

Early movies had too little character and plot to support a book-length treatment, but the length of movies quickly expanded from the one- and two-reelers of the nickel-odeons. Some of them went from ten minutes to four hundred and ten minutes. We don't think of them this way, but the multi-chapter movie serials were longer than almost all single-showing movies to follow, except for a few experimental pieces. (*The Irishman*, subject to gibes from every late-night comic about its interminable length, runs a mere 209 minutes.) With endless, twisting plots, a cavalcade of characters, and cliffhanger endings at the end of each chapter, movie serials were far closer to books on screen than any of the contemporary attempts to film famous novels or plays. (When Adolph Zukor started his production company in 1912, he publicized it with the slogan "Famous Players in Famous Plays." His first movies, all adaptations of plays, were four-reelers, or about 40 minutes long.)

Novelizations of movie serials start early, like with the very first serial. *What Happened to Mary?*, a title guaranteed to bring 'em back to theaters every month for a year of episodes, was made by the studio of canny Thomas Edison. The man who understood that the real money was in city-wide electrical systems,

Stage Struck front and back covers.

with lightbulbs only the visible tip of the iceberg, imbued his employees with the will to search out every possible stream of revenue. Horace G. Plympton, manager of Edison's New York motion picture studio, approached Charles Dwyer, editor of the magazine *The Ladies' World*, with a plan. Plympton would write a serial novel to run in twelve issues of the magazine and create a connected series of movie shorts to accompany each segment. The cross-publicity would be tremendous.

If something can work beyond the wildest imagination (doubtful: my imagination is Uncle Scroogean) *What Happened to Mary?* became a prime example, both in the short term and the long term. The heroine hounded through a series of harrowing adventures launched the plots of dozens of classic serials. Even without the cheating cliffhanger endings, a later invention, *Mary's* suspense

built up from month to month and the country went wild. Plympton and Dryer boosted the hysteria by attaching the first magazine chapter, "Escape from Bondage," to a contest announcing "One Hundred Dollars For You If You Can Tell 'What Happened to Mary'" in the second episode. Unprecedentedly, a stage play by Owen Davis debuted in New York *before the serial ended*. A sequel, *Who Will Marry Mary?*, kept the suspense going, opening just a month after the other ended.

And a novelization by Robert Cameron Brown became the very first movie tie-in in 1913, published by Grosset & Dunlap (G&D), which quickly became the dominant name in the field. (Tie-ins were then called "Photo-Play Editions," with hyphen, which appeared in newspapers as early as 1914, shortened to "Photoplay Edition" the next year.) Motion pictures were mass art, beloved by

Other Women's Husbands front and back covers.

the lower classes, scorned and ridiculed by the literary elite. Photoplay Editions weren't for the mainstream book crowd; they aimed at the same readers that bought dime novels and pulp magazines by the millions. That audience had little extra money to spend. G&D had formed in 1898 to do inexpensive hardback reprints of nonfiction books but found even bigger success with a novel, *Janice Meredith*, in 1899. They expanded their list to include cheap original juveniles, including the Hardy Boys and Nancy Drew series. Cheap hardback Photoplay Editions, ground out by the nearest hack writer, made perfect companions to their other titles. Many other firms jumped in, and virtually all based their releases more or less on the same template of dust jacket with colorized illustration, many stills from the production on glossy paper, and pictures of the cast, bracketing a

narrative on low-grade paper stock.

Cheapness remained primary. As G&D would learn in the 1940s, a 25¢ paperback outsold a $1.00 hardback reprint by an order of magnitude. Skipping the expensive boards for cheap paper covers was a notion that had occurred to entrepreneurs as soon as rotary presses capable of huge volumes for the masses appeared in the mid-19th century, starting with the nickel and then dime novels. In the decades before the mass-market-sized Penguin and Pocket Books editions took over the market in the late 1930s, paperbound releases were normally about the size of the book pages themselves. Therefore, most of the paperbound books of the time were what we today call digest sized.

Some of the earliest digest-sized Photoplay Editions came from J. P. Ogilvie & Co. Ogilvie started his first company in 1878 with a distin-

Above and right: Interior photographs from *Other Women's Husbands.*

guished partner, Francis S. Street, the Street in Street & Smith. After Street died, Ogilvie concentrated on "railroad literature," fast, light reading suitable for railroad passengers.

The Play Book series published 169 titles between 1903 and 1923, all novelizations of popular stage plays. Most were written by Grace Miller White, an impressive enough record

HOLDING THE HANDKERCHIEF IN HER HAND, SHE LOOKED AT DICK IN INQUIRY

"THE MOST WONDERFUL GIRL IN THE WORLD."

made more so because the majority of titles appeared before 1910.

Ogilvie also published the forthrightly-titled Railroad Series. "These are all large books, three-quarters of an inch thick, bound in paper covers in colors with separate cover designs on each," explained an ad. They probably could have been priced by the pound since weight and heft were their selling-points, but in fact cost 25¢ (later raised to 35¢). A contemporary ad lists Photoplay Editions mixed in with the regular novels. The movies novelized all appeared in the mid-to-late teens: *The Clemenceau Case*, *The Bondman*, *She*, *The Scarlet Letter*, and *20,000 Leagues Under the Sea*. The date of the book I found the ad in is uncertain, as it's a later undated edition of a 1903 title, but a similar listing appears in a known 1919 reprint. These books are impossible to find. Not even a cover popped up in an image search.

Very similar were the Street & Smith Picture Play Editions. Virtually nothing can be found about them except for a couple of stray titles. Arnie Davis, in his comprehensive *Photoplay Editions and other Movie Tie-In Books: The Golden Years 1912–1969*, lists *Around the World in 80 Days* as No. 20 and another edition of *The Bondman* as No. 5. However, the Verne movie adaptation was released in 1914 but *The Bondman* not until 1916. Whether this is a mistake in transcription or whether the books were printed well after the movie (as occasionally happened) is not clear.

They were not alone. An early attempt to start a digest line of Photoplay Editions came not from below but from the stars up high.

Douglas Fairbanks, one of the earliest genuine superstars, wanted more control over his pictures' financing. In 1919 he joined fellow superstars Mary Pickford (his wife), comic Charlie Chaplin, and director D. W. Griffith in founding United Artists. Fairbanks thought like Edison and wanted pieces of all profit streams. The Douglas Fairbanks Picture Corp. issued Photoplay Editions of Douglas Fairbanks motion pictures, including *The Three Musketeers* in 1921 and *Robin Hood* in 1922. They are digest-sized but, at only 40 pages, they're more like chapbooks than books. (Some of the hardback Photoplay Editions reached 300 pages.)

The breakthrough came via Jacobsen-Hodgkinson (J-H), a New York company that apparently was created for the express purpose of printing paperbound, digest-sized Photoplay Editions, which it called the "Popular Plays and Screen Library." (Despite the name, I can't find any record of a play novelization.) It was a spinoff from the Jacobsen Publishing Co. Inc. (Jacobsen), formed in New York in 1925 to publish, G&D-like, hardback reprint editions of popular novels. (Not related to an earlier Jacobsen Publishing Company in Chicago that dealt with trade magazines.) Series were a publishing fad at that time (Ogilvie had more than two dozen) and sure enough Jacobsen's reprints soon were grouped under a Modern Reprint Library banner. Jacobsen later, under The Fiction League imprint, also published new novels. Going wherever the money was, they issued a few unclassifiable oddball paperbacks, including *Numerology Simplified* and *Irish Come-All-Ye's: A Collection of Popular Song*

Ogilvie's Popular Railroad Series

88 SOPHIE LYONS, QUEEN OF THE BURGLARS........Lyons
89 REPENTED AT LEISURE
                    Bertha M. Clay
90 A GOLDEN HEART
                    Bertha M. Clay
91 A MAD LOVE....Bertha M. Clay
92 DORA THORNE...Bertha M. Clay
95 CUSTER'S LAST FIGHT
                    Grace Miller White
96 GIPSY BLAIR, THE WESTERN DETECTIVE...Judson R. Taylor
97 A TEXAS COWBOY....................Chas. A. Siringo
98 ANOTHER MAN'S WIFE................Grace Miller White
100 THE DUKE'S SECRET....................Bertha M. Clay
101 THORNS AND ORANGE BLOSSOMS...Bertha M. Clay
102 A BROKEN WEDDING RING...............Bertha M. Clay
105 TEMPEST AND SUNSHINE.............Mary J. Holmes
106 THROWN ON THE WORLD.............Bertha M. Clay
107 LENA RIVERS.......................Mary J. Holmes
108 THE CLEMENCEAU CASE (Photoplay Ed.)Alex. Dumas
109 THE BONDMAN (Photoplay Edition).........Hall Caine
110 WIFE IN NAME ONLY.................Bertha M. Clay
111 THE CATTLE RUSTLERS OF WYOMING Ford Douglass
112 SHE (Photoplay Edition, Illustrated).....H. Rider Haggard
113 THE SCARLET LETTER (Photoplay)....N. Hawthorne
114 20,000 LEAGUES UNDER THE SEA (Photoplay)..Verne
115 ON A MEXICAN MUSTANG THROUGH TEXAS
116 CAMILLE (Photoplay Ed., Ill.) ....Alexander Dumas
117 FRED BENNETT, THE MORMON DETECTIVE,
                    U. S. Marshall Bennett
118 THE WOMAN STEALER... ....Harry Mills
119 TORPEDOED IN THE MEDITERRANEAN....Johnson
120 WHICH LOVED HIM BEST............Bertha M. Clay
121 BETWEEN TWO LOVES..............Bertha M. Clay
122 THE ROBBER KING..................Patrick Tyrell
123 THE BUNCO STEERERS..............Inspector Murray
124 THE UNMARRIED MOTHER.......Florence Edna May
125 BEYOND THE LAW.............Emmett Dalton

Any of the above books are for sale by newsdealers everywhere, or they will be sent by mail postpaid, upon receipt of PRICE, 35 CENTS.

J. S. OGILVIE PUBLISHING COMPANY, 57 Rose St., New York

The Pace That Thrills front and back covers.

Classics - Sheet Music with Lyrics.

Photoplay Editions were introduced at the end of 1925. If the date of the copyright registration means anything, the first J-H novelization was *Stage-Struck: A Story of Love, Comedy and Pathos*, by Frank R. Adams, registered on November 20, 1925. (The title page of the book and the copyright registration show a hyphen; the wrappers lack one as did the original movie.) If Love, Comedy, and Pathos weren't enough, the front cover was filled with a pensive profile photo of Gloria Swanson staring meaningfully into the middle distance. Even better, the back cover had six Swansons, in character in six roles. J-H picked a biggie for their debut. Gloria Swanson was a super-star rivaling the United Artists gang, making $20,000 a week, or about a thousand times the average viewer's salary. Actors always love the tour de force of playing multiple roles, and Adams' story

gave her the juiciest of parts. As a poor Ohio waitress, she dreams of becoming an actress because the fry cook she has a crush on is besotted with them. Her dreams come true, figuratively and literally, with the help of the film's director, Allan Dwan. A major name himself, he created an extravaganza on screen, with the first and final scenes—set in the real world of Ohio rather than the fake world of the stage—filmed "in one of the most gorgeous pieces of [two-strip] Technicolor work ever done," said a newspaper review.

The firm couldn't have been an outsider trying to ride the coattails of fame. *Stage Struck* debuted in larger cities on November 13 so if J-H had the novelization ready to go by November 20, it must have worked closely with Paramount Pictures to coordinate the twin openings. The stills undoubtedly came directly from Paramount's publicity office. It's unthinkable that

The Calgary Stampede front and back covers.

Frank R. Adams had anything to do with the words, though. He was another big name, "one of America's best-known magazine writers" and author of several novels, who got the story credit for ten films in the 1920s. Some anonymous hack was given the screenplay and told to turn it into an approximation of prose.

I doubt it took long. The Popular Plays and Screen Library novelizations didn't give readers much for their money. The J-H books were a standard 134 pages of large print with large spaces between paragraphs. (The words ended on page 135 with a blank verso in the beginning and later a list of titles), but there wasn't a page 1 or 2: a title page backed with a copyright page were followed by Chapter 1 on page 5. Why J-H did this mystifies me.) Depending on how much dialog was invented, their length averaged only 20–25,000 words.

On the other hand, buyers didn't need to part with much money. The books cost a thin dime. For that, readers were also treated to three of the glossy full-page stills.

The novelizations were instant successes, at least if you believed J-H. Most news that came out of the movie business was in the form of press releases, reprinted essentially verbatim by outlets then as now hungry for any scrap of movie and star news. "Facts" have to be treated with the utmost suspicion. With that caveat, the January 16, 1926, *Motion Picture World* reported that "[The books] have a tremendous circulation, for they are on sale in all five and ten-cent stores in the country and in every railroad station in which there is a newsstand, besides thousands of regular book stores." And maybe that was true. Several of the early J-H books I have are second editions, announced as such

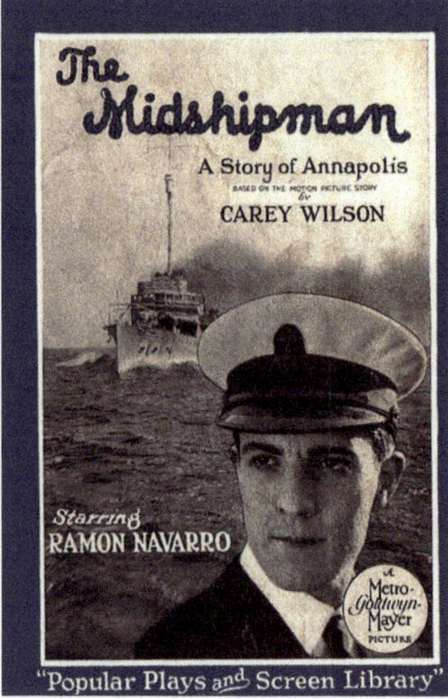

The Midshipman front and back covers.

over a list of other titles, a back page that the true 1925 first editions lack.

That same release also trumpeted that "Warner Brothers have effected an exploitation tie-up" with J-H, with the first release to be the tantalizingly-titled *Other Women's Husbands*, a now lost picture starring Monte Blue and Marie Provost. The IMDb doesn't even have a description of the plot, but one is available at my fingertips. (Exploitation didn't always have the negative connotation it almost universally displays today. The Cambridge English Dictionary gives a more neutral commercial definition as "the use or development of something for profit or progress in business.")

With Universal and Warner Brothers as partners in exploitation, J-H was already a major player. That understates their influence. Six novelizations were registered in 1925. *Stage-Struck* was from a Paramount film. One was a First National Picture (*The Pace That Thrills*), one a Universal (*The Calgary Stampede*), and three were by Metro-Goldwyn-Meyer (MGM). (Articles stated that the novelizations would be released monthly, although that seems not to have be true in practice.)

Proof of a 1925 deal with MGM is surprising, because that deal wasn't announced via press release in *Motion Picture World* until 1926. The short article in the January 2 issue used very similar language to the Warner Brothers announcement. "An exceptional exploitation tieup [sic] has just been affected [sic] by Metro-Goldwyn-Meyer." The first photoplay would be *The Midshipman*, with "the novelized version already being off the press," that being one of the 1925 registrations. (The others from MGM were *Old Clothes*: a sequel to the *"Ragman,"* and Tod Browning's *The Mocking*

Old Clothes front and back covers.

Bird, a renaming of *The Blackbird*.) "When one considers the wide distribution and selling outlet afforded by the powerful Woolworth, Kresge and McCrory stores such novelization of M-G-M current pictures is almost sensational." Super-colossal!

For whatever reason, that arrangement didn't last long. By September *Variety* revealed that Woolworth was now the "exclusive selling agents" reaping a "bonanza." Somebody was making a lot of money off them but it wasn't the studios. "There are small royalties to the film companies from whose production the stories are written, they considering it publicity." And as for the hacks, well, "Flat sums are paid the authors, who receive no credit."

Production ramped up to meet demand. About two dozen books, presumably two a month, were released in 1926. Few of these titles will strike sparks even in silent movie buffs today; the movie studios ground them out as much as the novelizers did. A couple did hit the jackpot. *Don Juan*, with swoon-inducing John Barrymore playing essentially himself, made the top ten grossing film list for 1926 and *Tell It to the Marines!* was the highest-grossing film of Lon Chaney's career, a December 1926 release and so a top ten in 1927. Not many of those contemporary stars who got the front covers to themselves—Reginald Denney, Hoot Gibson, Laura La Plante, Thomas Meighan, and little Jackie Coogan—successfully jumped to talkies. A sharp eye will spot several future superstars on the rear covers, though, including Myrna Loy and Joan Crawford as well as future Hollywood columnist Hedda Hopper. Almost all the covers have a blue frame around the central picture, but exceptions exist. Some examples, not exhaustive: *The Road*

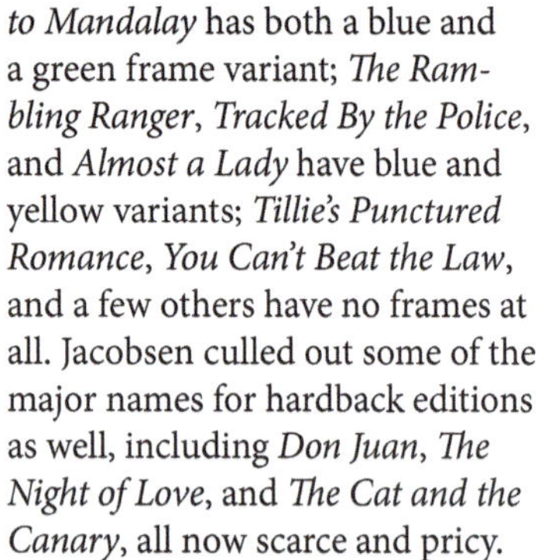

The Rambling Ranger front and back covers.

to Mandalay has both a blue and a green frame variant; *The Rambling Ranger*, *Tracked By the Police*, and *Almost a Lady* have blue and yellow variants; *Tillie's Punctured Romance*, *You Can't Beat the Law*, and a few others have no frames at all. Jacobsen culled out some of the major names for hardback editions as well, including *Don Juan*, *The Night of Love*, and *The Cat and the Canary*, all now scarce and pricy.

About halfway through the year, J-H had the money to correct a flaw in their competitiveness. Most of the hardback Photoplay Editions came with a colorized dust jacket. J-H started with black & white wrappers. These were sometimes striking stills from the movies but too often drab headshots of the stars. With the bonanza pouring in, J-H upgraded step by step. Mid-summer releases like *That's My Baby: A Story of Comedy, Thrills and Suspense* and *Take It*

From Me! gained red-orange overlays with eye-catching warm glows. Late in the year, *The Fire Brigade: An Epic Story of the Heroes of Peace* presented the heroic Charles Roy backed with a wall of red flame and gave the cowering heroine a dress with a yellow panel. *The Rambling Ranger: A Thrilling Romance of the Wild West*, released in April 1927, has an even more thrilling image of Jack Hoxie rescuing his cowering maiden from a runaway stagecoach. Most rear covers stuck to a standard format of a half-dozen headshots of the cast but a few had more interesting stills from the movie and *The Cohens and Kellys* superimposed complete body cutouts of the stars against the backdrop of a building.

Color improved the look, but didn't manage the necessary feat of being as enticing as the glossy movie magazines that were in the same price range. The cover of *Ranger* is

"Popular Plays and Screen Library"

"Popular Plays and Screen Library"

obviously a drawing and the firemen on Brigade are cut-outs over drawings. Over the next three years J-H upped its game. Covers on *Street of Chance*, with William Powell as a sad-eyed gambling addict, and *The Campus Flirt: A Captivating College Miss*, with a winking Bebe Daniels, rivaled or beat the magazines. *Bride of the Desert* in 1929 and 1930's *Let's Go Native* looked as good as the posters in a travel agency. For sheer exploitation in the negative sense, nothing else J-H ever did compared with the cover for *Body and Soul: A Tense Dramatic Story*. Tense? The cover shows Aileen Pringle being branded by a red-hot poker wielded by the fiendish Lionel Barrymore! Not surprisingly, this is one of the most expensive J-H books to buy today.

A word for collectors. J-H novelizations are a tiny niche in the gigantic Photoplay Editions collectibles market. Paperbound photoplays were a tiny percentage of the genre until the mass-market-sized paperbacks started flooding the market in the 1940s. Those eventually became so standard to any big-budget release that collectors scorned them. Emile Petaja's and Rick Miller's early guides to Photoplay Editions left out all paperbound editions. Moe Wadle's *The Movie Tie-In Book: A Collectors Guide to Paperback Movie Editions*, confoundingly starts in 1939 and therefore doesn't mention a single J-H novelization. Only Davis' book, a mammoth doorstop with 6100 entries and several thousand scanned covers on glossy paper, includes older digests, including J-H releases (which dropped the Hodgkinson half of the name in 1929).

The early titles, i.e. up through 1926, are not as rare as you might think, probably because they were produced in staggering numbers. You can find them in good to very good condition for $10–50. The major exception is *Tillie's Punctured Romance: A Love Comedy of Circus Life*. An unlovable remake of an earlier film and play, the movie stars W. C. Fields as the bad guy ringmaster. Nevertheless, with his face on the cover, the J-H edition is a prize for fanatical Fields collectors. It's listed online for $650, topping even *Body and Soul*.

Completists will drool over two hard-to-find associational items. The first appeared probably in 1926 to accompany the now lost serial *Fighting with Buffalo Bill*. Jacobsen created a paper cutout "movie theater" for kids. I found a description online at <Eclectibles.com>.

An uncut paper movie theatre with the characters from "Fighting with Buffalo Bill" a 1926 American Western film serial (totaling over four hours) staring [sic] Wallace MacDonald, Edmund Cobb and Elsa Benham. The paper theatre consists of the original carrying envelope, a movie theatre set with a curtain, a landscape background, one sheet of characters, and one single fold instruction page that includes a verse about men roaming the plains. On the character sheet there nine characters [sic] that one can cut out and fold at the dotted line in order to make them stand on their own. Of these nine characters, four stand-alone men, one stand-alone woman, three men on horses (two of which are Native Americans) and one man standing behind a teepee. The scenes and curtains are in black and white. The characters are black and white images from photographs,

presumably of the characters from the movie. The envelope the movie theatre comes in, incorrectly states that there are 10 characters to play with. This was presumably a printing mistake as the 10 has been crossed out and a 9 was written in.

Undated, but probably from the 1930s since it uses Jacobsen's later 61 East 11th Street address rather than the 1440 Broadway of the 1920s, is a set of twenty-four 5" x 7" movie star photo cards. It's not clear whether these were part of a promotional tie-in with a product or a package that one could buy as a whole. The names are an almost literal snapshot of the transition from silent stars to sound stars with Vilma Banky, John Gilbert, William Haines, and Claire Windsor alongside Janet Gaynor, Gary Cooper, and Ronald Colman.

Compared to the glory year of 1926, 1927 in hindsight betrays clear signs of the beginning of the end. Only half as many titles were released and each following year the number dropped even more. A combination of factors probably ganged up on them. The market was flooded with Photoplay Editions, with G&D and A. L. Burt filling bookstores with titles. Woolworth might have been the best store to have an exclusive deal with—the equivalent of an exclusive Walmart deal today—but the loss of Kresge and McCrory meant that about 800 outlets disappeared, a significant loss for an impulse-buy item. Keeping circulation high was the only way to amortize the increasing costs of color covers. Worse, Kresge teamed with rival "five & dime" store chain Kress to jointly publish a photoplay magazine, presumably in retaliation. Jacobsen fought back with the *Jacobsen Movie Novel Magazine,* which put out four issues in 1929. Davis describes these as digests that are "taller" and "slightly larger" than the previous series. They contained only 94 pages but if they were bigger and used smaller type, as would be normal for magazines, they could easily fit the same number of words.

Worst of all, the very rationale for Photoplay Editions started to fade. Their heyday paralleled the rise of short films into full-length motion picture extravaganzas. Viewers didn't need to buy a book to fill in the nuances of a ten-minute melodrama. Slapstick was a worse sell: it couldn't be transferred to the written page at all. Nobody made a Photoplay Edition of a Charlie Chaplin movie. By the 1920s, though, movies had scripts that imitated stage plays in complexity. A few interstitial cards couldn't sufficiently convey the plot and dialog as well as a full written story.

Talking pictures filled in those mental gaps, putting the words right in the mouths of one's favorite stars. No anonymous hack could emulate that. The handful of talkies that were released in 1927 quickly proved themselves at the box office, despite the wobbling sound and static camerawork. *Don Juan* scored big because it had a musical background, even if no spoken dialog. Hollywood flipped itself in the fastest reworking of an entire industry maybe ever. Silent movies were shown in tens of thousands of theaters across America. All, except for those in the smallest towns, had installed sound technology by 1930. Jacobsen released its last title in 1931, or maybe 1932. By then it called its

series "Screen Hit Novels." To keep the company going, Jacobsen apparently tried desperately to cut costs and increase revenue. The price increased to 15¢. The page count was cut to around 100. Interior stills were left out. As always, the public refused to buy more of a now inferior product. *The Robert D. Fisher Manual of Extinct or Obsolete Companies* for 1937 includes Jacobsen-Hodgkinson and lists a 1934 date.

A check at Biblio and Abebooks showed that 30 of the 33 titles from 1925 and 1926 are listed but only 19 of the 44 from 1927 on, and those later titles tend to command higher prices, usually from $75 up. Condition makes a huge difference; the pulp paper crumbles at a touch. Davis says there were "ninety odd titles," but that includes variants like the hardcovers and the movie magazines. He has 77 J-H or Jacobsen paperbound digest-sized books listed. Two notes. *The Call of the Klondike* was listed as forthcoming in a back-of-the-book ad, but seems never to have appeared. Similarly, something called *The Play Must Go On* is mentioned as the subject of the fifth issue of the magazine but I can find no such movie with that title ever being made. Davis doesn't have either and it would amaze me if anybody else had a full set.

If you're interested in dabbling in them, you can often pick up a lot of a random dozen of the early books for around $100, as I did on eBay, and then decide if you want to fill in around them. If you want to get serious, I've prepared what seems to be the only listing of every known title.

As a bonus, I've also included a listing of the known Photoplay Novel digests in the

classic era of 1938-1958.

Since that time, the occasional random digest Photoplay Edition has been released but Davis stops his listing in 1969 and Wadle in the early 1990's, when it was published, so no book or online site mentioned covers the last full quarter-century. There's a project for a film fanatic!

Jacobsen-Hodgkinson Photoplay Digest Editions 1925-1932(?)

Title of book	Author of screenplay	Studio[2]	Date	Publisher[3]
Almost a Lady	Frank R. Adams	M	1927	J-H
Body and Soul[1]	Katherine N. Burt	MGM	1927	J-H
Bride of the Desert	Arthur Hoerl	R	1929	J
Broken Hearts of Hollywood	Raymond L. Schrock & Edward Clark	WB	1926	J-H
Calgary Stampede, The	Raymond L. Schrock	U	1925	J-H
Call of the Klondike	[unknown]	R	1928	J-H
Campus Flirt, The	Louise Long	P	1927	J-H
Cat and the Canary, The[1]	John Willard	U	1927	J-H
Cat Creeps, The	John Willard	U	1930	J-H
Cohens and the Kellys, The	Aaron Hoffmann	U	1926	J-H
Cohens and the Kellys in Paris, The	Alfred A. Cohn	U	1928	J-H
College Love	Leonard Fields	U	1929	J
Cossacks, The	Lyof N. Tolstoi	MGM	1928	J-H
Crimson City, The	Coldeway Anthony	WB	1927	J-H
Dance Madness	S. Jay Kaufman	MGM	1926	J-H
Derelict, The	William Slavens McNutt & Grover Jones	P	1930	J
Devil's Circus, The	Benjamin Christianson	MGM	1926	J-H
Divine Woman, The[1]	Gladys Unger	MGM	1928	J-H
Dixie Flyer	H. H. Van Loan	R	1926	J-H
Don Juan[1]	Inez Sabastien	WB	1926	J-H
Don't Tell the Wife	William B. Courtney	WB	1927	J-H
Fire Brigade, The	Robert Lee	MGM	1926	J-H
Forbidden Hours	Younger A. P.	MGM	1928	J-H
Forbidden Waters	Charles Logue	Metro	1926	J-H
Hawk's Nest, The	Wid Gunning	FN	1928	J-H
Hero of the Big Snows	Edward Adamson	WB	1926	J-H
Hurricane	Norman Springer	C	1929	J
Illicit	Eve Bernstein	WB	1931	J
Irresistible Lover, The	Evelyn Campbell	U	1927	J-H
Jazz Mad	Svend Gade	U	1927	J-H
Kiki	Norma Talmadge	FN	1926	J-H
King of the Jungle	William E. Wing	R	1927	J-H
Les Miserables	not given	U	1926	J-H
Let's Go Native	Dorothy Farnum	PP	1930	J
Love Thief, The	Margaret Mayo	U	1926	J-H
Madonna of Avenue A, The	Mark Canfield	WB	1929	J
Man Who Laughs, The	Paul Gulick	U	1928	J-H
Melody Man, The	Howard J. Green	C	1930	J
Menace, The	[unknown]	C	1932	J
Midnight Sun, The	Holger Lundberg	U	1925	J-H
Midshipman, The	Carey Wilson	MGM	1925	J-H
Mighty, The	Robert Lee	P	1930	J
Mississippi Gambler, The	Karl Brown & Leonard Fields	U	1929	J
Mocking Bird, The	Tod Browning	MGM	1926	J-H
New Klondike, The	Peggy Griffith	P	1925	J-H
New York	Barbara Chambers & Becky Gardner	P	1927	J-H
Night Cry, The	Edward Adamson	WB	1926	J-H
Night of Love, The[1]	Lenore J. Coffee	UA	1927	J-H
Old Clothes	Willard Mack	MGM	1925	J-H
Other Women's Husbands	E. T. Lowe	WB	1926	J-H
Outside the Law	Tod Browning	U	1926	J-H
Pace That Thrills, The	Robert Weber	FN	1925	J-H
Perils of the Coast Guard	John Francis Natteford	U	1926	J-H
Play Girl, The	J. Stone	Fox	1928	J-H
Quarterback, The	Welles Root	P	1926	J-H
Rambling Ranger, The	George Hively	U	1927	J-H
Redemption	Dorothy Farnum	MGM	1930	J
Resurrection	Finis Fox	U	1931	J
Road to Mandalay, The	Tod Browning	MGM	1926	J-H
Sensation Seekers	Ernest Pascal	U	1927	J-H
Side Street	Mal St. Clair & George O'Hara	RKO	1929	J

Continued

Jacobsen-Hodgkinson Photoplay Digest Editions 1925-1932(?)

Title of book	Author of screenplay	Studio[2]	Date	Publisher[3]
Stage Struck	Frank R. Adams	P	1925	J-H
Street of Chance	Oliver H. P. Garrett	P	1930	J
Streets of Shanghai	John Francis Natteford	T/S	1928	J-H
Take It from Me!	Will Johnstone & Will R. Anderson	U	1926	J-H
Tell it to the Marines	E. Richard Strayer	MGM	1926	J-H
That's My Baby	George J. Crone	P	1926	J-H
Tillie's Punctured Romance	Joan Weber	P	1925	J-H
Tracked by the Police	William Courtney	WB	1926	J-H
Undertow	Wilbur D. Steele	U	1930	J
Vengeance	F. Hugh Herbert	C	1930	J
Vice Squad, The	Oliver H. P. Garrett	P	1931	J
Wall Street	Jack Kirkland & Paul Gangelin	C	1930	J
What Happened to Jones	George Broadhurst	U	1926	J-H
Where East Is East	Tod Browning & Drago Harry Sinclair	MGM	1929	J
Why Girls Go Back Home	Catharine Brody	WB	1926	J-H
You Can't Beat the Law	H. H. Van Loan	R	1928	J-H

Movie Novel Magazine 1929

Title	Author	Studio	Date	Publisher
Dream of Love	Dorothy Farnum	MGM	1929	MNM4
His Private Life	Ernest Vadja & Keene Thompson	P	1929	MNM2
Man, Woman, and Wife	Charles Logue	MGM	1929	MNM3
Sins of the Father	Norman Burnstine	P	1929	MNM1

Notes: Book titles are occasionally different from the movie titles.
[1] Known additional hardback edition
Welles Root is the way the author is credited on *The Quarterback*; his first name was actually spelled Wells.
[2] C=Columbia Pictures; FN=First National Pictures; Fox=Fox Film Corporation; M=Metro Pictures; MGM= Metro-Goldwyn-Mayer Studios; P=Paramount Pictures; R=Rayart Pictures; RKO=RKO Pictures; T/S=Tiffany/Stahl Productions; U=Universal Studios; UA=United Artists
[3] J=Jacobsen Publishing Co., Inc.; J-H=Jacobsen-Hodgkinson Corporation
MNM=Movie Novel Magazine

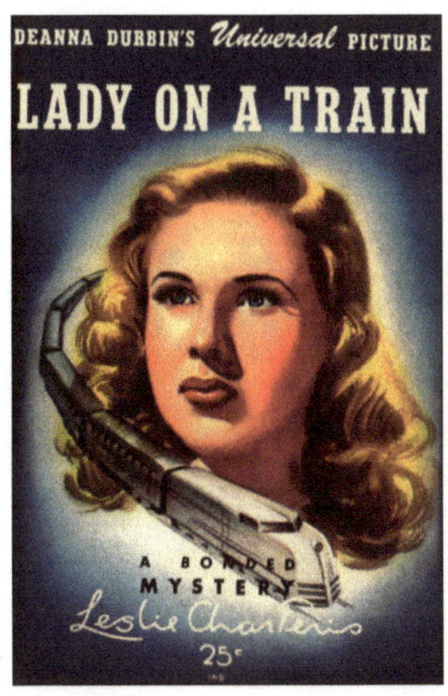

1938-1958 digest Photoplay Edition novels

Title of book	Author credited	Publisher	No.	Studio[1]
Adventures of Buffalo Bill, The	Col. William F. Cody	Boblin Sales Co.	NN	20
Build My Gallows High	Geoffrey Homes	Jonathan Press	35	RKO
Dark Corner	Leonard Q. Ross	Century	31	20
Fallen Angel	Marty Holland	Century	26	20
Frightened Child, The	Dana Lyon	Mercury	158	20
Jackie Robinson Story, The	Arthur Mann	F. J. Low	NN	J
Lady on a Train	Leslie Charteris	Bonded Books	NN	U
Make Haste to Live	The Gordons	Bestseller	170	REP
Murder Makes a Detective	Samuel Michael Fuller	Bestseller	143	C
Secret Command	John Ward Hawkins	Adventure Novel Classic	22	C
Singapore	William G. Bogart	Century	37	U
Tall in the Saddle	Gordon Young	Western Novel Classic	42	RKO
20 Million Miles to Earth	Henry Slesar	Amazing SF Novel	NN	C
Vice Squad	Leslie T. White	Bestseller	165	UA
Without Reservations	Jane Allen & Mac Livingston	Century	103	RKO

Notes: Book titles are often different from the movie titles.
Bonded Books put out three issues of its digest-sized *Movie Mystery Magazine* in 1946 and 1947, which included a novelization along with other material.
[1]20=20th Century Fox; C=Columbia; J=Jewel Pictures; REP=Republic; RKO=RKO Pictures; UA=United Artists

New articles by **Steve Carper** appear regularly on <FlyingCarsandFoodPills.com>. Steve's book *Robots In American Popular Culture* and companion website of the same name are essential reading. His digest novel collection has passed 1300, not even including *Photoplay Editions*.

Paperback Fanatic No. 43
Review by Richard Krauss

A special edition on Gold Medal paperbacks. Not a history of the publisher, but a more personal and idiosyncratic view of some of its legendary titles.

Published in January 2020, the 43rd issue of *Paperback Fanatic* opens with editor Justin Marriott's "Fanatical Thoughts," a recap of his recent trip to the UK Paperback Fair in November 2019. Although a London fair is a bit far for most of his readers in the States, his excitement is representative of attending a good show of this type, meeting friends old and new and finding treasures to buy or simply peruse.

Gold Medal Reviews

Reprinted reviews of Gold Medal titles from the website <Paperback Warrior.com> offer a little background on authors, detailed synopses (thoughtfully avoiding spoilers), and a final verdict on each entry. Titles include: *Backwoods Tramp* by Harry Whittington, *Black Wings Has My Angel* by Elliott Chaze, *Color Him Dead* by Charles Runyon, *Devil in Dungarees* by Albert Conroy, *Don't Get Caught* by Carter Cullen, *Drive East on 66* by Richard Wormser, *The Killer* by Wade Miller, *The Late Mrs. Five* by Richard Wormser, *Madball* by Fredric Brown, *One for Hell* by Jada M. Davis, *The Scarred Man* by Basil Heatter, *So Young, So Wicked* by Jonathan Craig, *The Specialists* by Lawrence Block, and *Tears are for Angels* by Paul Connolly.

The quality of the reviews should incent you to follow the Warrior website if you're not already onboard. Enjoy more reviews online or subscribe to the Paperback Warrior Podcast.

Gil Brewer the Dark Invader
by Paul Bishop

Bishop delivers a fine article on Gil Brewer, deftly weaving his personal experience of the author's work with Brewer's tragic biography, and synopses of a few of his most successful novels. The piece is beautifully illustrated with a generous collection of cover images, in one case highlighting different editions of the same novel: *The Red Scarf*.

Brewer's Droop by Justin Marriott

By the 1970s, most of Brewer's output was written under pseudonyms and house names for lower-rung publishers like Priory

and Five Star. Marriott highlights a few covers from this era in this two-page spread, including one novel featuring series character Harry Arvay, an Israeli secret agent.

Brewer in the MAMs by Bob Deis

A six-page pictorial, displaying various opening spreads from Men's Adventure Magazines that ran "condensed" versions of

Brewer's earlier novels, often with truncated or doctored titles. Their accompanying paintings reveal some smokin' hot eye candy— mostly in black-and-white.

The Other Marlowe by Paul Bishop

This fascinating overview of the tragic noir writer, Dan Marlowe, exposes his personal demons and downhill slide from his most famous Gold Medal triumph: *The Name of the Game is Death*. On the success of this hardboiled classic, Marlowe revamped its protagonist, Earl Drake, and launched a series of follow-on paperbacks. They sold, but sales slowly eroded and Marlowe found himself working for less lucrative markets, eventually writing under pseudonyms and house names. The article includes a gorgeous sampling of cover images from many of Marlowe's best.

A Town Called Malice
by Justin Marriott

In this supplement to Bishop's article, Marriott provides a detailed, two-page review of one of Marlowe's best remembered novels, comparing his work to John D. MacDonald. "This 'fish out of water' theme is present in *The Vengeance Man*, albeit flipped, as Wilson is a sociopath and murderer trying to make his way in the world of legitimate small-town politics."

Charles Williams and His Girls
by Rob Matthews

Another Gold Medal master gets his due in Matthews' well-researched tribute that skillfully combines biography with synopses of several of the noir author's best-loved novels. Cover art abounds, including UK

Pan editions, Dell, and reissues under alternative titles. An Ed Gorman quote from the article: "Line by line Williams was the best of all the Gold Medal writers…" Matthew also provides an impressive Williams bibliography that includes every edition and alternate title he could uncover.

A Visual Guide to Robert McGinnis by Justin Marriott

Twenty-six gorgeous examples of Robert McGinnis' cover artistry, from 1958 through 2007, are displayed along with a crisp synopsis of each book as well as Marriott's observations on each paperback's cover and why he selected it.

Brighter than Salmon Pink
by Justin Marriott

Even on vacation, an original paperback fanatic is hard at work devouring books for his next article. In this case, the works of John D. MacDonald. Marriott provides an excellent overview of a handful of the bestselling author's novels including *The Damned, Darker Than Amber, You Live Once, Dead Low Tide*, and *The Executioners*—basis for the classic *Cape Fear* movies. Marriott summarizes the plot of each and thoughtfully places them along the writer's journey.

Wyatt Doyle Interviewed
by Justin Marriott

Robert Deis and Wyatt Doyle are the force behind New Texture's Men's Adventure Library, a series that explores Men's Adventure Magazines (MAMs) from the 1940s through the early 1970s. Marriott's interview with Doyle centers on two recent releases: *Eva* devoted to

MAM supermodel Eva Lynd, an actress and model who often posed for MAM cover paintings and illustrations; and *Mort Kunstler, The Godfather of Pulp Fiction Illustrators.*

"Generally, we create most of our books in two distinct editions, with different cover art: Trade softcovers for those with a casual interest in the subject, and expanded, deluxe hardcovers with additional material for the collector."

Summary

Paperback Fanatic No. 43 provides a satisfying glimpse into Gold Medal's roster of talented authors and the challenges they faced to continue writing for a living as the markets changed. Its expansive pages provide ample space for a dazzling collection of cover images—all in vivid, lurid color. An excellent issue of this beloved collectors' magazine.

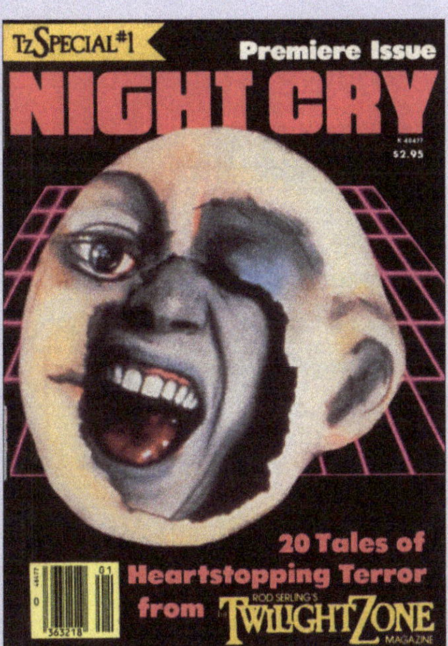

Night Cry Vol. 1 No. 1 Jan. 1984.
Cover photo by Rosie Mackiewicz

Night Cry*
TZ Publications, New York, NY
Eleven issues
Vol. 1 No. 1 (Jan. 1984) to
Vol. 2 No. 5 (Fall 1987)
Quarterly beginning with Vol. 1 No. 2
(Summer 1985)
Chairman/Executive Publisher:
S. Edward Orenstein
Assoc. Publisher/Consulting Editor:
Carol Serling
Executive Editor: John R. Bensink
Editor in Chief: T.E.D. Klein
Managing Editor: Robert Sabat
Assistant Editor: Alan Rodgers
Design Director: Michael Monte
Art Director: Patti Mock
5.5" x 7.5"
194 pages
$2.95 cover price

Rod Serling's The Twilight Zone Magazine's Digest Specials (First issue only)
The staff roster above is for issue No. 1, several staff changes occurred over the course of the magazine's run.

7" x 10" 300 pages
McFarland Books, June 2019
Trade Paperback and Kindle

Companion Website
<robotsinamericanpopularculture.com>

PULPFEST
Celebrating...
MYSTERY, ADVENTURE, SCIENCE FICTION, AND MORE
WITH FARMERCON
AT THE DOUBLETREE BY HILTON HOTEL
PITTSBURGH — CRANBERRY IN MARS, PA.
AUG. 5-8, 2021
PulpFest.com   PulpFest   @PulpFest   PulpFest
Artwork by MARGARET BRUNDAGE for WEIRD TALES (October 1933)

Opening Lines

Selections from the digests featured in this edition.

"We checked on the van in the back of the Walmart parking lot shortly after the second body surfaced near Turkey Creek."
"Creepy" by Alec Cizak
Lake County Incidents October 2019

"There was a lot of grumbling, but I managed to get everyone to come with me into the attic, where I turned on the light, revealing the Rillian I had found eating out of the garbage the night before."
"Aid and Comfort" by J. Manfred Weichsel
EconoClash Review No. 5 January 2020

"Among the people of the Floats caste distinctions were fast losing their old-time importance."
"The Kragen" by Jack Vance *The Most Thrilling Science Fiction Ever Told* No. 12 Spring 1969

"On the last night she was sure of being human, Imani dreamt of the river."
"The River" by Alice Towey
Asimov's Science Fiction May/Jun 2020

"They were singing it now, just as he had heard it sung along the great canals—not openly so that they could be identified—but in isolated groups lost from view among the smouldering rubble of the shattered town."
"Last Days of Thronas" by John Bloodstone
Science Stories No. 3 February 1954

"'Damn it, Joey,' Sylvia said as she slapped his ass. 'Do it again.'"
"Three Brisket Tacos and a Sig Sauer" by Michael Bracken *Guns + Tacos* Season 1 Episode 2 2019

"Beth watched her Mama pat the top of the grave down with the rusty shovel."
"Nodding Angel" by John Shirley
Weirdbook No. 42 March 2020

"The Universal Press Service Building was a squatty chunk of stubborn granite, set down defiantly amid the airy structures of downtown New York."
"The Goddess of World 21" by Henry Slesar
The Most Thrilling Science Fiction Ever Told No. 11 Winter 1968

"Macklin was near the end of his endurance—and of his sanity—when the emergency party from First Colony arrived."
"Tiger's Cage" by Roger Dee
Science Stories No. 4 April 1954

"What happened was, the TV in the next room heard my girlfriend and me arguing and called the police."
"Net Loss" by James Sallis
Analog May/Jun 2020

"The zipper in Captain Bunnell's sleeping bag jammed and that gave the gorilla a head start on him."
"Dream Girl" by Ron Goulart
Fantasy & Science Fiction December 1958

"His was the only car in either direction, three-thirty a.m. on the Antelope Valley Freeway, driving north above L.A., heading for a week at Lake Tahoe, then a new life in San Francisco."
"Weigh Station" by Robert Crais *Rod Serling's The Twilight Zone Magazine Digest Specials* aka *Night Cry* Vol. 1 No. 1 January 1984

"She'd been tweeting about her literature professor, Dr. Lipsek, who'd had the audacity to bring vanilla ice cream to class the day before fall break."
"The People in the Margins" by Alec Cizak
Lake County Incidents October 2019

"There is no gainsaying that the Solomons are a hard-bitten bunch of islands."
"The Terrible Solomons" by Jack London
Tales of the Sea Vol. 1 No. 1 Spring 1953

"The future of the world is a political problem, with statesmen and philosophers and plunderers holding sway."
The City in the Sea by Wilson Tucker
Nova SF Novels, 1954

"Moran, naturally, did not mean to help in the carrying out of the plan which would mean his destruction one way or another."
"Planet of Dread" by Murray Leinster
The Most Thrilling Science Fiction Ever Told No. 10 Fall 1968

"Three blocks away and the lights are like cigarettes burning through a black blanket."
"Three Chalupas, Rice, Soda . . . and a Kimber .45" by Trey R. Barker
Guns + Tacos Season 1 Episode 4 2019

"Mr. John Waterfield reached the limit of the edible nail on his left small finger and moodily switched to the other hand."
"Special Jobbery" by H.B. Fyfe
Astounding Science Fiction Sept. 1949

"Isis squeezed her pistol's warm trigger and her shot hit the man five yards in front of her between the eyes."
"These Violent Delights" by Mandi Jourdan
Pulp Modern Vol. 2 No. 5 June 2020

"The merchant Calaphais was coming to an agreement with the seller of dates, Mustapha of Caesarea, when their negotiations attracted the notice of the demon Malchance."
"Calaphais and the Demon Malchance" by John Shirley *Weirdbook* No. 42 March 2020

"He was a bookish-looking guy with an air of having been beaten down without realizing it."
"Nantucket Undertow" by Shelly Dickson Carr *Ellery Queen Mystery Magazine* May/Jun 2020